# STUFF

## Jeremy Strong

*Illustrated by Seb Burnett*

GALAXY
*G*
PLUS

First published in Great Britain
in 2005
by Puffin Books
This Large Print edition licensed and published by
BBC Audiobooks
by arrangement with
Penguin Books Ltd 2009

ISBN: 978 1405 663205

Text copyright ©
Jeremy Strong, 2005

British Library Cataloguing in Publication Data available

Printed and bound in Great Britain by
CPI Antony Rowe, Chippenham and Eastbourne

*This is for my son, Daniel. I know you're thirty now, and Sam is only one, but it won't be long before he is a teenager. I hope this might remind you. And by the way, you weren't a bit like Stuff, so you can't sue.*

This book was a new venture for me and I could not have written it without advice and/or encouragement from my wife, Susan, and daughter, Jessica; and from Patric Netscher and Debbie Moody—massive thanks. The book also required tender administration and suggestive remarks from Yvonne Hooker at the Puffin Mother Ship, and several other crew members—big thanks for your patience and tolerance and for letting me get away with it.

I am also hugely indebted to the following younger readers: Will Mulder, Dru Shearn, Alex, Ashley and Joe. Finally my thanks to the teenage reader I met in Lancashire who told me I should write something funny for teenage boys, and to Louise Rennison, whose Georgia Nicolson stories got me thinking, gave my wife and myself a lot of laughs, and encouraged lip-nibbling. Don't try this at home. (Unless your parents are out.)

# CONTENTS

1. About Tasha's Knickers 1
2. Frogs and Trifles 4
3. Hugging Aliens 11
4. How My Universe Was Changed 16
5. Behold—Skysurfer! 20
6. Radical Rabbit 25

Punykid's Battle with the Drooling
Dorkoids! I

7. Two Dead Famous People 31
8. Running Away—First Attempt 37
9. Refuting Mr Teddy 41
10. Running Away—Second Attempt 44
11. Shock! Horror! 48
12. Very Useful Lists 53
13. How to Embarrass Yourself 58

Punykid's Battle with the Drooling
Dorkoids! II

14. Darcy 61
15. The Grange (creepy stuff) 66
16. Darcy Again 70
17. Decision Time 74

Punykid's Battle with the Drooling
Dorkoids! III

18. Egg Whisks vs Burglars                    79
19. Running Away—Third Attempt                85
20. My Best Friend?                           90
21. Time to Come Clean                        94

Punykid's Battle with the Drooling
Dorkoids! IV

22. Happy Home                                99
23. Running Away—Fourth Attempt              104
24. More Revelations                         110
25. Toilet Trouble                           114
26. Chugga-chugga!                           120

Punykid's Battle with the Drooling
Dorkoids! V

27. Holy Sock!                               125
28. Destiny Makes a Move                     129
29. Toothbrushes and Other WMDs              133
30. Stuff I Didn't Know                      139

Punykid's Battle with the Drooling
Dorkoids! VI

# ABOUT TASHA'S KNICKERS

'You've been going through my knicker drawer, Simon.'

'No, I haven't!'

'So, how come this happened?' Natasha waved her undies at me.

'I didn't do it,' I lied.

'Oh yeah, like who else would? You've been in my room rifling through my knickers.'

'I did not go rifling through your stinky knickers.' And, believe me, I was telling the truth. Natasha's room was, after all, way beyond the Pit of Despair. In fact, it was probably the Garbage Can of Crudgirl. 'They were in my room. *Your* mum put *my* clean clothes in *my* room on *my* bed and in among them was a pair of *your* undies. Right?'

That shut her up for five seconds, but only five and then she was off again.

'Yeah? And then this magic writing just appeared on them, did it?' Natasha waved the little white panties at me. I tried not to smile. They were dinky pants and I'd been astonished—not to mention embarrassed—to discover them among my pile of laundry in the first place, but there they were, and while they were there I thought I might as well examine them. As you do. Well, you would, wouldn't you? Go on, be honest, you would. I hooked a finger at each end of the waistband and looked at them. Very dinky.

The front panel was dotted with little printed hearts. Above them was the word HEARTS, printed in red. I had an idea. Oh yes, it was a good one. All I did was, I got a dark-green felt tip and turned the pants over. Then on the back I drew puffs of cloud and above them I carefully printed the word FARTS.

I'm going to be Damien Hirst when I get older. Well, obviously not *the* Damien Hirst because Damien Hirst is already Damien Hirst, if you get my drift. I'm going to be *like* him. Famous artist. (But better at drawing.)

Anyhow, I thought it was funny. It *was* funny. Hearts and Farts. It wasn't my fault if Natasha hadn't brought her sense of humour with her when she came to live in our house. It wasn't even as if I'd asked her to come and live with us. Nobody had even thought to ask me, yet here she was, prancing about the place as if she owned it. She's only been here a month. I've been here fourteen and a half years! She's lived here twenty-seven days, nine hours and forty-five minutes—approximately. Not very long, is it?

Proper house squatters have to live in the same place for years before they can claim it's theirs and that's all Tasha is—a squatter. She already thinks the place is hers. Even trans-universal invaders would have to stay longer than her before they could claim Earth. I can't see them arriving in our front room and saying, 'Earthlings, we come to live in your house and we have been here five minutes, so it is legally now ours. Please take your tatty sofa, your vegetable rack full of mouldy broccoli and your smelly bathroom towels and GO. But leave us the PlayStation and your computer games. We like

2

those.'

If aliens tried to pull that one, they'd be thrown out on their ears (assuming they had ears) by the International Court of Human Rights. And bear in mind that space invaders *might* come and live in your house. It could happen. Statistically speaking, there is a fifty per cent chance of finding life on other planets out there in the universe. What I advise is: be prepared, and know your legal rights. Also, hide the PlayStation before they arrive.

So, Tasha shouldn't be here. She *wouldn't* be here if it weren't for my mum going off with the Frog, and Dad bringing back Sherry Trifle. More of the Frog later—let's start with the Trifle.

Obviously Sherry Trifle is not my stepmother's real name, but that's what I call her and now you want to know why, so I shall tell you. The first time I ever saw her was when Dad brought her to the house a few months after Mum left. He had warned me first. That was kind.

'Simon, I'm going out and when I come back I shall have a lady friend with me.'

Honest to God! That's exactly what he said. Was I surprised? Yes. Why? Because my dad can hardly manage to go out and buy a pair of socks for himself, let alone find what he so politely called 'a lady friend'. So, how did he find her? I will tell you. He didn't. She found him and chatted him up, in the supermarket. She hypnotized him with her stunning blue eyes and stiletto heels. Not to mention the push-up bra.

'She dropped her bananas in front of me,' Dad explained. And when she bent down to pick them up I realized how lovely she was.' He reddened. 'We've been seeing a lot of each other. We like

3

each other, Simon. When I bring her back I want you to be nice to her.'

So off he goes and, of course, I'm hanging around by my bedroom window, peering out from behind the curtains like some curtain-twitching voyeur. I see Dad's car coming down the road. My heart's speeding up and my head's spinning. I don't know what's happening in my life and it's worrying. This woman could be my second mum— and I had enough trouble with the first.

The car stops outside and Dad's in such a hurry he almost falls out, stumbles, rushes round to the passenger door, opens it and out comes . . .

2

## FROGS AND TRIFLES

. . . a leg. A long, slim leg. Hmmm, this is different, if not interesting.

Two long, slim legs, with those hypnotic stiletto heels, and Dad's grinning from ear to ear and no wonder. Hell's bells! Mum never had legs like that. Mum got her legs from a furniture catalogue.

Then out she comes and . . . hell's bells with added gongs and stuff—it's a sherry trifle!

Honest, she was really just like a sherry trifle. She was wearing a red miniskirt, with a cream jumper, and perched on top of her head was a red beret, just like a cherry. And she was carrying a rabbit, a big rabbit not a cooking one—a pet. More on that later.

I don't call her Trifle to her face. I usually say,

4

oh so politely, 'dear stepmother'. Which she hates.
Dad hates it too.

'It's so . . .' he struggled.

'What?'

'It doesn't sound right,' he complained.

I can't see the problem but apparently there is
one. It's not my fault if she doesn't like it.

'Can't you call her Tracey?' suggested Dad.

'Dad, you've always told me to show respect to
old people. You said I shouldn't get personal with
the older generations, such as yourself and my
dear stepmother. So what's her proper name
—Mrs . . . ?'

'You can't call her Mrs Overdown!'

I opened my mouth, but Dad got in first.

'And you can't call her *Ms*, either!' he
interrupted. I could see murder creeping into his
eyes at that point, so I let the subject drop.
Anyhow, to me she'll always be Sherry Trifle.

'Just give her a chance,' Dad called after me.
'That's all I ask.'

And now you're probably wondering if I am ever
going to get round to explaining about the Frog,
and I'm going to tell you now because I am a fund
of information, which is why everyone at school
calls me Stuff. I'm full of it. (At least that's what
my French teacher thinks.)

Mum and Dad split up about a year ago. Mum
left and went off with this bloke I call the Frog—
and no, he's not French. He wears glasses that
magnify his eyes. I don't know what Mum sees in
him. Big eyes, I suppose. They remind me of frog
eyes, if you see them close up. Of course, you don't
often get the chance to see a frog close up, so
maybe you have no idea what I'm talking about,

5

but I had a frog experience when I was eight and I have never forgotten it.

## My Frog Experience

We've got a pond in the back garden and one summer I was lying on my stomach next to the pond and suddenly this monster frog came shlooping out from beneath the surface—and it was like it was in slo-mo, you know? It was like everything had slowed right down and I could see this huge frog zooming towards me from out of nowhere, with no warning, like some Giant Stealth Frog, its whole head getting bigger and bigger as it came straight at me. I could see a huge mouth and the eyes! As big as footballs. I thought the monster would swallow my head. Bat's buttocks!

Of course, the frog didn't. It just crashed into my face. SHPLAPP! Then its Happy feet went shlipp-plipp all over my head as it tried to get a grip and scrabble off me. I was struggling to get up and clawing at my face and eventually the frog leaped off and disappeared back into the pond. I've not seen it since, but I guess it's still waiting down there somewhere—Giant Stealth Frog, waiting to swallow my head.

**End of Frog Experience**

His real name's Martin. Not the frog's; Mum's boyfriend. Sorry, *man*-friend. That's what Mum said, the only time I've visited them so far. I am going to see them again, but they're up in Scotland, and that's not just round the corner, is it? Not from where I am, it isn't. It's round about 5,638 corners, not to mention the straight bits.

Mum does ring every so often.

'Martin's a man, Simon,' Mum said. 'Not like your father.'

Is that weird? What did she mean? *Not like your father.* Was she trying to tell me something? Was my dad a secret transvestite? That could be very interesting. Maybe she had some Polaroids I could sell at school.

'Mum, I thought Dad *was* a man.'

'Simon, he reads comics.'

'Mum, they're not comics. They're classics.'

'Simon, *Great Expectations* is a classic. *Treasure Island* is a classic. *Silver Surfer* and *Batman* are comics.'

'They're classic comics.'

Mum gave me a withering look. 'Comics,' she repeated. 'Picture stories. He's still a little boy'

'Why did you marry him in the first place, then?'

That made her think. 'Because when we got married I was a little girl,' Mum said eventually. 'I grew up. He didn't.'

And there you have it. The difference between Mum and Dad. I didn't argue any further. I knew what she meant, but she was only half right. Maybe it is odd that Dad collects comics, but they are valuable and some are brilliant. Dad's got piles of them. He buys them at boot sales and auctions and grotty antiquey-typey shoppeys. He's got fantastic early editions of *Superman* and *Batman,* really old comics from the 1930s and 1940s.

He lets me look at them as long as I handle them carefully. *Silver Surfer* is my favourite. He's a superdepressed superhero—well, he would have to be superdepressed, wouldn't he, being a superhero? Don't know what he was so depressed about. Maybe it was his diet. Broccoli depresses me. Maybe he was eating too much Really Big Broccoli for Superheroes—the broccoli that makes you GO!

Anyhow, Silver Surfer surfs the galaxies on his silver board. The artwork is terrific. I think maybe that's what I want to do—story pictures. I don't mean, like illustrating; I mean, telling the whole story through pictures. That's how I see things sometimes. I think it's got to do with Giant Stealth Frog when I was eight. It was seeing that frog coming at me in slo-mo, bit by bit, like each frame of a film, building up, building the whole story until SPLAPP! It was all over my face.

Anyhow, I like drawing. My friend Pete thinks I'm really good. What do you reckon? My art teacher reckons I could make it. Which is nice, because my maths teacher says I'm crap (his word, not mine), and Baguette, the French teacher (he's tall, thin and crusty—ha ha), just growls *'quel horreur'* into his beard every time he sees me. But I am good at art and I reckon it's because I spent so much time when I was younger trying to copy *Silver Surfer.* Now I make up my own things.

But I still haven't told you about Tasha, so here goes.

You can see what's coming, I expect. Dad and Sherry Trifle hit it off with one another and, to and behold, one day Dad tells me that Sherry Trifle is going to move in.

'So, what's the good news?' I asked, and he scowled.

'Don't be like that, Simon. Tracey is lovely and very kind. I'm sure you'll get to like her too. The extra-good news is that you'll have a friend.

8

Someone to talk to.'

'I don't want to talk to her. I don't want her to be my friend.'

'I don't mean Tracey,' said Dad, and you should have seen his face. S-M-U-G written in big letters right across it. He was so pleased he'd wrong-footed me. 'Tracey's got a daughter, Natasha. Same age as you. She knows what it's like.'

'Knows what what's like?'

Dad's eyes widened and he gave a little shrug. 'Everything. Splitting up, new parents. You know—everything.'

'Really?' (This said in my deepest, deep-frozen liquid-nitrogen tone of voice.)

Dad didn't look so pleased any more. Good. That'd teach him.

'You'll like her,' he said hopefully.

Well, Dad, you were wrong there, weren't you, because I don't like her one bit.

Natasha is foul. OK, so she looks all right, if she wears plenty of make-up, and she's got a cute bum, but she scowls all the time and stinks the place out with cruddy perfume. She flounces around, complaining about everything and blaming me or Dad for what's wrong with her life. She's driving me nuts and Dad won't do anything about it.

Sherry Trifle just smiles sweetly and says things like: 'We all have to live with other people we don't like, Simon.' Yeah. Exactly. She says it with a smile but you feel as if she's just made you swallow a porcupine. I tried to tell Mum on the phone and all she said was: 'You think you've got problems? Huh.' I could hear bagpipes in the background, but I don't think that had anything to with it.

The only people I can talk to about it are Pete

and Delfine. Pete's my best friend and he thought the hearty-farty pants were really funny, but then he doesn't like Tasha either. At least I don't think he does. He doesn't say much about it, but he frowns and stares at her a lot.

Delfine's my girlfriend and she says Natasha shouldn't be sharing a house with me at all. 'Why not?' I asked.

'She's a girl.'

'So?'

Delfine giggled. She's got a funny giggle, like someone ringing a little bell that's cracked, so it doesn't actually tinkle, it sort of *tunkles* instead, if you get my drift. 'You know what I mean,' she said. 'You might, you know . . .'

'No, I don't.' I was bemused.

Delfine tunkled again and then whispered, 'She might fancy you.'

'She's my stepsister.'

'I know, but . . .'

'And I can't stand the sight of her.'

'Oh, good.' Delfine smiled and snuggled up to me.

Honestly, that's Delfine for you. You may well ask why she's my girlfriend. Because she's cuddly and nice and I like her, that's why. And because I'd already asked three other girls and they'd all said 'no'. Anyhow, you've got to have a girlfriend—bit like having the right trainers. And I'm not being sexist or shoe-ist or anything. I just mean, you wouldn't be seen out without either of them. Equally important—see?

So, I asked Pete and Delfine what I should do about Natasha.

'Only one thing you can do, mate,' said Pete

seriously. 'Leave home.'

## 3

## HUGGING ALIENS

Badger's buttocks! It's all right for Pete to say things like that. He's lucky. His parents don't only live miles away from him, they're on the other side of the North Atlantic. They work in the USA because Pete's dad is some computer geek and over there he gets paid millisquillions. They didn't want to take Pete out of school, even though he wanted to go, so Pete lives here with his Aunt Polly, and she more or less lets him do what he likes. He comes and goes when he wants, stays up as long as he wants—he's even driven her car, which goes like stonk. *And* he gets to go to America once or twice a year. I mean, life is not fair, is it?

And then there was Dad. What would he do without me? I know La Trifle was keeping him well organized now, but she didn't understand him like I did. She'd made him pack all his comics away in the attic, for a start.

'I can't just leave,' I said.

Delfine tightened her grip on my arm. I sensed her panic. Delfine was prone to panic attacks. She'd see a worm—panic (wrigglyphobia). She'd see a tree—panic (treefallcrushmephobia). And that was just going home from school.

'Why can't you leave?' asked Pete. 'You could come and stay at my place.'

'Really?'

Pete's place! I suddenly felt like someone was opening the door of my cage and helping me out, like a wee hamster being released back into the wild. This could be great! Freedom! And Dad wouldn't be so far away—I could keep an eye on things. Then I remembered all those parties Pete kept telling me about, with wild goings-on. I mean, Pete and his aunt really LIVED!

Pete grinned. 'No probs. Don't suppose Aunt Polly would even notice. She's out most of the time. She's got a new bloke. Don't think he's much older than me.'

There was a horrified squeak from Delfine. 'A toy boy?'

'What's wrong?' laughed Pete. 'Be good, I reckon, going with an older woman. What do you think, Stuff?' Pete grinned and winked at me.

Delfine was staring at both of us. She thought Pete was serious, but I knew he was teasing. Pete's like that. He likes winding people up.

'Don't call him Stuff,' said Delfine.

'I don't mind,' I told her, and I don't. It's cool. My head's full of it. I don't even know where most of it comes from. I just seem to pick it up, like my brain emits a special sort of tracker beam that locks on to pointless information. For instance, do you know how many sausages were on board the *Titanic* when it went down? I do—about 20,000. Twenty thousand sausages drowned when that ship sank. What a tragedy. I like sausages.

Pete grinned again. He's always smiling, like life is such a laugh. Well it is, for him. And it would be for me too, if I went and lived at his Aunt Polly's. Pete said he'd seen her in her undies.

12

'She was hardly wearing anything,' he said. 'It was one of those thong things.'

'A thing-thong?'

'No,' said Pete, very seriously. 'A thong thing. Thing-thongs are different. Thing-thongs are very boring and have men with beards and guitars. Women in scanty panties wouldn't be seen dead at a thing-thong.'

So, going to live at Pete's was an attractive proposition. In more ways than one. I might even get to drive his aunt's car.

## Pete's Car Story

Aunt Polly's got a Subaru. Yep. Exactly. I heard your sharp intake of breath. Pretty neat stuff So, they're out in the Subaru—Pete, Aunt Polly and her boyfriend. Can't remember his name. Let's call him Roberto. Aunt Polly likes Italian men. And Swedes (the country, not the vegetable). Roberto said he'd show Polly how to do a handbrake turn and they go to this deserted car park and roar up and down doing whopping great skid-turns. And then Roberto leans across to Pete and asks him if he wants to try. (I told Pete I didn't think he could speak Italian. Pete said they used sign language, with sound effects added.)

Of course Pete wants a try. He climbs in the driver's seat and they're off. Pete said it was like being in a rocket! (I asked him how many times had he been in a rocket? He told me to go and do something unspeakable to my rear end, which wasn't very nice, was it?) Anyhow, Pete drove very, very fast—so fast that when he pulled on the handbrake the car didn't just do a

13

half-turn, it did one and a half revolutions.

'Wow!' I said.

'Yeah,' said Pete. 'It scared Roberto so much he threw up.' (Pete demonstrated this with more sign language and sound effects.)

**End of Pete's Car Story**

I was impressed. So, it seemed that living at Aunt Polly's could be the most exciting thing ever to happen to me.

'You sure she wouldn't mind?' I asked.

'She'd be too busy to even notice,' he repeated, and he turned his back, clasped his hands round himself and did that pretend smooching thing, making revolting noises. *Shlurrrrrrp!*

'You're disgusting,' murmured Delfine, looking away.

Pete gave me a despairing glance. 'It's too easy,' he murmured. 'I need someone more challenging.' He slapped my back. 'Gotta go. See you later.'

As soon as he'd gone Delfine got all serious on me. 'You're not going to Pete's, are you?'

'I'm thinking about it.'

'But you can't. What will your dad say?'

'He'll probably say, "Where are you, Simon?" But I won't hear him because I'll be at Pete's.'

'He'll be upset.'

'Delfy, *I'm* upset at the moment. Natasha and her mum are driving me mad. For God's sake, Tasha likes listening to Honzo da Bonzo! How can anyone like listening to Honzo da Bonzo?' Then I told her about the knickers.

'That's horrible,' she said.

'Why?'

'They could have been mine,' she said.

14

Excuse me? Was there any kind of logic in this? Emergency! Delfine's brain was flatlining—start brain-cell transfusion immediately.

'But they weren't yours,' I pointed out.

'They might have been.'

'How come? How would your panties get into my washing?'

Delfine turned so red her freckles vanished. 'I meant, maybe one day you might write something like that on my knickers.'

'I might, but only if you're wearing them,' I joked. Wrong move. Badly wrong. Bad, bad, bad. It took me ten minutes to calm her down. I had to get on my knees and say: 'I cross my heart and swear that I would rather die than write on Delfine Smith's knickers.' Lower eyes and allow short pause to show respect. 'Can I get up now?'

Delfine gave a wan smile and nodded. I sighed. She looked lovely when she smiled. She had such a nice mouth and wonderful, hazel eyes. It reminded me why I went out with her in the first place because, to be honest, it wasn't for her sense of humour.

When Delfine and I kissed each other goodbye I was glad we'd made up and I hugged her really tight, so I could feel her pressing into me. That's a weird sensation, isn't it? Like holding an alien. Not that I've ever held an alien, but you know what I mean. They're such a different shape, girls, and I never know where to put my hands. I know where I'd *like* to put them, but I reckon that if that's where I'd like to put them it's bound to be one of those interesting but no-go places where girls get all iffy-sniffy and bothered. Then there'd be more trouble. I'll have to try one day, though, just to see

15

what happens, just to see what it's like.

Delfine said, 'You're squeezing me.'

I put on a silly French accent and whispered in her ear, 'I vont to squeeze you to death becoz you are juz zo 'uggable.'

Delfine tunkled. I could feel the warmth of her body, smell her skin. Hmmm, school-soap smell. That was . . . unromantic, but clean.

'You won't go to Pete's, will you?' she whispered.

'I'll think about it,' I said, which was true, because I was already thinking about it and what I was thinking was: *I'm going to go to Pete's.* That'd show them. That'd make Dad sit up and think.

4

## HOW MY UNIVERSE WAS CHANGED

Then, next day, school—and something completely changed the universe as I knew it. Pete and I had art first thing—a double period. I was looking forward to it because it's the only good thing about school as far as I'm concerned.

I was the last to arrive. I'd had to make a detour to the loos for a spot check. Actually, it was much more than a spot, it was a major nose eruption. Overnight I'd acquired a pimple the size of Mount Etna and ready to blow. How did they manage to appear so quickly, so silently? It was as if great armies of acne lay hidden in dark corners, beneath carpets, behind wardrobes, in cracks and crevices, ready to leap out and ambush your sleeping body at night. They scuttle up walls, slide silently across ceilings and drop down upon prone teenagers. Splip, splap, splop.

Nasty, horrible stuff. And it had come at just the wrong moment. *(Is there a right time for acne? This is the question for today's television poll. Viewers— phone in your answer NOW!)*

It was certainly the wrong moment for me, because when I got to the art room there was a new student. Sky.

That was her name. Sky.

Quiet pause to call up image.

Close your eyes and think warm, summer thoughts. Think of that deep, deep blue you get on a really clear day, not a cloud in sight, and you can feel the soft warmth in the air, maybe a touch of gentle breeze, and you feel on top of the world and everything is so gorgeous you feel as if you're actually breathing in beauty. That's how I felt when I first saw Sky.

She was stunning. Gorgeous. She was almost as tall as me, willowy, with short, spiky hair the colour of dark straw, and a kind of lopsided, dyed-blonde streak that made her look like some elfin superhero who'd escaped from a computer game. It began at the nape of her neck, curved and climbed up the right side of her skull, over her ear and then angled over towards the centre of the hairline, just above her eyes.

Her face was just lovely. You know that story about Helen of Troy, who was so beautiful her face 'could launch a thousand ships'? Well, Sky's could launch ten thousand. In fact Sky's face could have raised the *Titanic* and saved all those sausages, if the *Titanic* had been interested in women. Which

17

it wasn't, because it was a ship. At any rate, you get the point. My English teacher says that this kind of writing is called a 'digression' and it's pointless and I shouldn't do it. I said it wasn't a digression, it was a point of interest. Not to me, she said. But you're not writing it, I said, all jolly, like. And you're in detention, she said, for cheek. Bummer. How my life goes.

Back to Sky and her face: green, exotic eyes that seemed to speak of far-flung places. Her mouth had the most kissable lips on Planet Earth. Her skin was like glowing honey—flawless.

Pete was already chatting her up. He would be. He was perched on the desk next to her, swinging his legs casually, looking so cool I could have killed him.

'So, where are you from?' I heard him ask.

'Wolverhampton.'

'Is that on Mars somewhere?' laughed Pete.

'Is that a joke?' she answered.

When Delfine says something like that it usually means she's cross. But when Sky said it, it was like she was telling Pete she knew it was a joke, but it wasn't very funny, although she didn't mind, but please think of something better to say next time. And Pete couldn't think of anything, so he had to shut up. It wasn't often that Pete was left semi-stunned.

I stood at the back, listening and watching. I had to take several deep breaths. Sky really was something. This girl was having a strong physical effect on me. It wasn't only the way she looked, it was the way she held herself and the calm way she answered all the questions, like nothing could rattle her. She glanced at me a couple of times,

18

probably because her eyes were drawn to my giant spot. She seemed alert to everything.

Matters were only brought to a halt when our art teacher arrived. Miss Kovak got the picture at once and took control.

'Break it up, everyone. I want the girls here and the boys over there. You've obviously all met our new student, Sky.'

General sniggers from one side.

'Yes, thank you, boys, do try and raise your thoughts to higher planes this morning. Please make her feel welcome. OK, everyone, we shall be working on life studies for the next few weeks.'

'Will that be drawing the human body?' smirked Nathan Wilder.

'Yes, Nathan, it will, and to answer your next question: no, Nathan, it will not involve drawing naked women.'

More sniggers.

'What about naked men, Miss Kovak?'

This came from Hayley Jenks. It set most of the girls whooping. Hayley must be the crudest girl I have ever met, but more on that would be a digression and not just for cheek this time, so, sorry. Maybe another time. (Let's just say I wouldn't like to meet her down a dark alley)

Miss Kovak gave a tolerant smile. 'I have no idea, ladies. Perhaps we should ask.' She turned to us. 'Would any of the gentlemen care to pose?'

'Gerroff!' That was a scandalized Pete.

Miss Kovak clapped her hands. 'I thought not. Maybe we can get down to some work instead. Portraits from life—working in pairs, taking it in turns to draw each other. I want girl/boy pairs as far as possible and, since it would appear that the boys rather foolishly all wish to partner poor Sky, we shall sort this out by letting the girls choose their partners.'

We all protested loudly, but Miss Kovak called on Hayley to make the first choice.

'Pete,' she said, with a little giggle.

Pete plunged to his knees, hands clasped. 'Miss Kovak! This isn't fair!' he pleaded. 'Save me!'

'All you have to do is draw each other,' Miss Kovak pointed out. 'Nobody asked you to marry her, Pete.'

Pete stuck two fingers down his throat.

'Aw, he's so disgusting, Miss,' complained Hayley. 'Can I choose someone else?'

Miss Kovak laughed. 'Off you go. Sky—your turn.'

## 5

## BEHOLD—SKYSURFER!

That really perked up the boys. Charlie got out his comb. Karl smoothed his hair. Harry ruffled his. They smiled at Sky—well, leered anyhow. There were loud whispers of 'Me!' and 'Hey, Sky, over here!'

I felt like I was being pulled towards her, like she was my destiny. We would meet—it was inevitable. The Hand of Kismet had written it in the Book of Fate. Awesome. I didn't know her. We hadn't even spoken to each other. Now she was scanning eager faces. I casually placed my hand in front of my spot and hoped the pulsing glow of radioactive acne couldn't pass through my skin. Maybe Sky could now see my hand as an X-ray?

'Sky?' prompted Miss Kovak. 'Of course, you don't know anyone's name, do you? Just point, that'll be fine.'

Sky raised her arm and everyone began to push.

'Boys, it's no good trying to stand where Sky is pointing. Just keep still, thank you. OK, Sky, go ahead.'

'Him,' she nodded.

I picked up my pencils and sketch pad and off we went, leaving the Hounds of Envy to howl their annoyance. Ha ha ha, sorted! We settled in a quiet corner near the windows, where the light was better. My heart was thrumming.

'I don't know your name,' Sky said.

'Sorry. Simon. Stuff. People call me Stuff.' And I explained why.

'I like that,' she said.

'Why did you pick me out of that lot?'

'Don't get big-headed about it,' said Sky, with a faint smile. 'That was easy. You're the only one who hasn't been forcing yourself on me since I walked into the room.'

'Right.'

Another little smile. She cocked her head on one side and her eyebrows gave a little flicker. 'And I like the way you look. I don't mean your appearance, I mean the way you look at people, as if you're trying to see the person inside.'

'Right.'

Mad panic. Oh God, she talked about scary things. This was way beyond the kind of stuff Delfine and I did. All we did was slag off Honzo da Bonzo, among others. Could I handle this? I mean,

21

this was deep like, I dunno, philosophy or something.

Sky angled her pad on her lap and started to draw. The minutes slowly passed and I began to relax. This was good. All the time she was concentrating on her pad I could study her. I couldn't believe she was so close. Her face was so neat, as if God had drawn it with a really fine pencil.

That is so stupid! I don't even believe in God and here he is, not just drawing—he's drawing the Love of My Life!

It is so difficult, so hard to explain, but I'm trying to capture everything I loved about her—the high cheekbones, the graceful slant to her green eyes, her cheerful little knees.

Well, they were! As soon as I saw Sky's knees they just seemed to smile at me.

Anyhow, I was getting desperate to start drawing her. I had such an image of her in my mind and it was bursting to leap on to the page. It was the only way to show how I saw her, what I saw in her.

Sky lowered her pad. 'Done,' she said, with a broad smile.

Miss Kovak came over and glanced at the portrait. 'That's good, Sky. Did you do much art at your last school?'

'Not really, but I've always drawn, ever since I was about three. I'm going to be an artist.'

Miss Kovak nodded. 'I'd say you're heading in the right direction. You'd better show Simon. He's dying to see.'

Sky blushed slightly, lifted her pad and turned it round. It was terrific. It really looked like me.

'What do you think?'

'It's good, but you could have left out my spot. Is my chin really that big?'

Sky laughed. 'It's not big. It's your chin, that's all. Come on, your turn now.'

I began to draw and, as I sketched, the real world shut down around me. I was drawing my way into another universe. I drew and drew and the art room vanished and Sky and I were left floating in a timeless world of our own, a world of hidden dangers. Half the time I didn't even look at her, as if my pencil had a mind of its own. And what I was drawing didn't make sense. I wasn't just drawing Sky, I was drawing this new world. Bit by bit she took shape on the page in front of me, bursting with life, with power. And she wasn't just a face— she was AN EPIC!

*In a Time that doesn't exist, a different world is born . . .*

*Great galaxies collide. Black holes swallow entire solar systems. Wormholes wriggle between parallel universes.*

*Danger is everywhere, in the shape of monstrous creatures unknown on Earth, creatures more hideous than Mr Frobisher, the IT teacher, more dangerous than a female tyrannosaurus with PMT—this is the world of the Drooling Dorkoids of Doom.*

*Yet in this world of death and despair there is still hope. One superhuman strides across Space, bringing hope to all those who suffer.*

*Behold—Skysurfer!!*

*POW! KERRUNGG! SPLOGG! PLIFF!*

'My goodness!'

It was Miss Kovak, standing behind me, studying my work. She drew a deep breath and let it out slowly. 'Hmmm. That person being eaten by a shark there—is that your English teacher?'

'Um, sort of.'

Miss Kovak nodded slowly. 'It's quite something, Simon. Is that how you see Sky?'

I wanted the ground to swallow me up. 'It's—just how it came out,' I explained.

Sky looked puzzled.

'You'd better show her,' Miss Kovak suggested.

I lifted up my pad and turned it round. It felt as if my embarrassment was so great it had jumped right out of my body and infected hers. I watched Sky turn red.

'Wow!' she murmured, and no wonder.

Her eyes flicked to mine and quickly looked away, but already I had seen amazement and fear. I cursed myself for getting so carried away.

'Simon, could you bring your work over here for a moment, please?'

Now I was going to cop it from Miss Kovak too. Great. I picked up my pad and followed her to the other end of the room, where we couldn't be heard. Miss Kovak never did public put-downs. Not like some in the school who I could mention. Now she took another long look at the drawing. 'I didn't know you did work like this,' she began.

'I only do it at home. I got carried away. Sorry.'

'But it's terrific. I don't think it will get you through the art exam, but it has great impact.'

I was speechless. Inside my head everything was going crazy. I waited breathlessly to hear what she would say next.

'I have an idea for you to consider. First of all,

24

you mustn't show this to anyone else. OK?'

'But Sky's already seen it.'

Miss Kovak glanced towards Sky. 'I think I can sort this with her. Do another portrait, an ordinary one this time—not quite so . . . exciting. You can show that to the others. Then come and see me at the end of the lesson and I can tell you what I've got in mind.'

I could see the rest of the group were getting interested in what was going on. Pete was pulling faces. He obviously thought I was in deep trouble.

'What about the picture I've already done?' I asked.

Miss Kovak winked at me. 'We can soon sort that out.' She suddenly raised her voice and tore a clean sheet of paper from my pad. 'And don't you ever make a drawing like that again, Simon. Is that clear?'

'Yes, Miss Kovak.' I hung my head and grinned at my shoes. I still hadn't a clue what was going on, but it was great!

Miss Kovak ripped the clean sheet to bits and put them in the bin. 'Now, go back and do another portrait—a decent one.'

The boys at the other end of the room hooted with delight.


6

RADICAL RABBIT

Miss Kovak put out a school broadsheet every week. She called it *Art Works*. It had illustrations, poetry and short stories by students. Now she wanted me to add a graphic story—a comic strip, with a storyline. Miss Kovak was working on a degree project, trying to show different ways of bringing art to more people.

'I want to show everyone that art isn't a hobby. It's something relevant to all of us because it is about our own lives. It speaks to everybody.'

'Right,' I said, and tried to look intelligent. She'd given me a lot to think about. Her idea was exciting—off the wall, even. I wondered if I was good enough to do it. Could I come up with enough ideas? Making drawings was one thing, but adding words and a storyline—that would be hard.

I loved the secrecy, as if we were doing something naughty. I knew we weren't because Miss Kovak had given it the OK, but it *was* secret, and it made me grin inside.

'You could draw a comic strip for *Art Works* and let it tell a story,' Miss Kovak said. 'It could be about your life, your feelings . . . about school. I loved the little details, like the shark. Heaven knows what that *Titanic* business was about, but I expect you do! And the way you caught Sky's character—it was as if you'd seen something brave and exciting and adventurous inside her that nobody else could see, but you found it and turned it into a different character, but who was also the same.'

'Yeah.' (?????? What was she on about!? I was just drawing!)

Miss Kovak smiled and patted my shoulder. 'Don't worry, Simon, that's just the smart talk I'm going to put in my degree thesis. You come up with the artwork and we'll take things from there. Don't

26

tell anyone. It'll be anonymous, and that means you have a free hand to draw what you like. I want to see how people react.' Miss Kovak looked me straight in the eye. 'I want it to make a stir. Get the message?'

Then, as I was leaving, she added a bit more. 'You know, if you can catch Sky like that, you might be able to do it for others in the school. Think about it.'

So I was. Thinking about it.

Of course, at the end of the day Pete wanted to know what was going on, so I told him Miss Kovak had been really cross, that was all.

'What did you draw? Why did she tear it up?'

'Doesn't matter.'

'You drew Sky in the nuddy!'

'Come on! I'm not that stupid, not in the middle of an art lesson.'

'Well, it must have been something pretty bad,' Pete insisted.

'Look, it was just a crap picture. She told me I was wasting my time and if I couldn't be bothered to make an effort I should give up art altogether.'

Pete walked beside me in silence for a bit, but he could never keep his mouth shut for long.

'So, not in the nuddy?'

'No!'

'Just undies?' he asked hopefully.

'Pete!'

'Oh, all right. Pity really. See you tomorrow.' And he peeled off down the road to Aunt Polly's.

I was barely inside my own front door when my feet were subjected to a wild assault from a manic white furry tornado. Pankhurst was up to her usual tricks.

27

I had better explain. You remember when Sherry Trifle arrived she brought a rabbit with her, and at the time I said there would be more info about the rabbit later? Well, now is later and here's the info.

## Some Useful Information About Emmeline Pankhurst

Emmeline Pankhurst is a giant angora rabbit. (Well, obviously Emmeline Pankhurst was not a giant rabbit originally—she was an Edwardian lady who protested about women not being allowed to vote by chaining herself to railings and things like that, as you all know.)

Pankhurst (the rabbit) is enormous, about as big as a fluffed-up pillow and a great deal more terrifying. To be fair, Tasha did tell me.

'She's a radical feminist rabbit and she doesn't like men. Don't say I haven't warned you.'

'That's stupid,' I snapped. (This was barely five minutes before Pankhurst hurled herself from an armchair and did a drop kick on my behind that cannoned me halfway across the room—and left two dirty great bruises on my posterior.)

'See,' said Tasha, tossing her curls. Miss Smug, 2005.

Later on I stood in the bathroom and examined my backside in the mirror. (As you do.) I wondered what would happen if I got run over and killed and ended up on a slab in the mortuary. The doctor is examining my dead body and he (or she—cheeky thing!) looks at my bum and says: 'Aha! Cuts and abrasions to the buttocks, made by large paws. Good grief! This poor young man was mown down by a giant hit-and-run rabbit.'

Dad and I soon discovered that Pankhurst would attack us at any time, anywhere. She never ambushed women, only men. *It was as if she'd been trained.* Spooky. We began to creep about the house like the SAS on a deadly mission. Meanwhile, Pankhurst had the run of the place.

'Dad, we're being ruled by a rabbit. Do something. Get rid of it.'

'Si, if I get rid of the rabbit, I will lose Tracey.'

'So, what's the problem?'

'I will pretend I didn't hear you say that, Simon.'

'And I will pretend that Pankhurst hasn't just weed in your slippers, Dad.'

At least Dad had the guts to make a complaint.

'She's a house rabbit,' Sherry Trifle declared. (So, no apology there, then. What a surprise.) 'She's always lived in the house.'

'That's disgusting,' I complained.

La Trifle cocked an eyebrow 'She's a lot cleaner than most men I know.'

'I've never seen men weeing in their slippers,' I pointed out.

'Be careful, Simon,' warned La Trifle. 'You're so sharp you'll cut yourself.'

So, I got home from school, walked through the door and Pankhurst was upon me, pounding my feet with her enormous paws. You are probably thinking: *So what? It's only a rabbit. You* have obviously not been reading this properly. Remember that word 'giant'? Remember how it came before the word 'rabbit'? Pankhurst weighed as much as a small refuse truck and here she was, trying to turn my feet into mash. It was not pleasant.

I dashed for the stairs, but Pankhurst was too quick. She scampered round me and threw herself across my path so that I tripped and made a short, unpowered flight across the hallway before crashing on to the bottom of the staircase. Painful? Yes. But it did give me a good idea for a brand-new extreme sport: indoor hang-gliding.

But that was not the end of it. The rabbit thundered up the stairs after me and I only managed to save myself by slamming my bedroom door shut on the monster. Pankhurst headbutted the door so hard it almost came off its hinges. I collapsed on my bed and nursed my feet. What I say is, give rabbits the vote and stop all this nonsense.

A strange day. It felt as if I had been turned upside down and given a good shake. Or maybe it was my world that had been turned upside down. Either way *something* had been turned upside down and shaken.

First of all there was Miss Kovak's secret project. It sounded great and I wanted to start work on it right away. I just wasn't too sure how.

Then there was Sky. Couldn't stop thinking about her. I really, really wanted to know her better, to be friends with her.

And, of course, there was Delfine. What would happen there? I didn't want to do the two-timing thing. It wasn't right. And Delfine really loved me. I know she got cross with me sometimes but that was *because* she loved me. I knew that because she kept telling me, so it would be hard on her if I dumped her and hard for me to do. Did I love her? No. I liked her. She was good to be with, panic attacks aside. But Sky was the Real Thing.

30

So, if I chucked Delfine and went after Sky, what would happen if I failed? I wouldn't have anything. Result: misery.

If I stayed with Delfine and went after Sky behind Delfine's back, what would happen if I got Sky? I'd have to tell Delfine. Result: misery.

If I stayed with Delfine, went after Sky behind Delfine's back and didn't get Sky? Result: misery.

If I stayed with Delfine and just stared at Sky every day? Result: more misery.

And if Delfine ever found out what I was thinking right at this moment? Mass suicide, probably.

It seemed to me that things were about to get awfully miserable. How my life goes.

I decided to take my mind off Delfine by starting work on the secret project.

## 7

## TWO DEAD FAMOUS PEOPLE

Killer day at school—brilliant. Miss Kovak loved the strip. Said it was just what she was looking for.

'I'm glad you've disguised Sky's appearance a bit. There should be a bit of mystery about her. Who's this monster woman?' She pointed at La Trifle.

'It's, um, it's . . . just . . . something that came into my head,' I mumbled.

Miss Kovak let it go. 'You've got an interesting imagination,' she said. 'Have you ever seen the paintings of Salvador Dali? Look him up. He was a surrealist. I think he might appeal to you.'

So that's what I did next. It had been odd seeing Miss Kovak like that and handing over the strip—all had to be done where nobody could see—very undercover. *The name's Stuff. James Stuff. 0071/4. Licensed to draw.* Anyhow, off to the library and I found a book on Salvador Dali and the surrealist painters.

## A Brief History of Salvador Dali
Salvador Dali was a Spanish artist. He lived near Barcelona and he died in the 1980s. He became famous for three reasons.

1. He had a weird moustache.
2. He made weird films, with things like ants crawling out of wounded hands.
3. He painted weird, dreamlike pictures of things like elephants on stilts, melting watches and a steam train thundering out of a front-room fireplace. (Actually that last one was by another surrealist painter, Magritte. He was in the same book. His stuff was even more brain-exploding—especially the man with an apple for a head.)

Dali liked to shock people. He also liked to paint naked women. What a surprise. Like I said before, I'm going to be an artist when I leave school. I thought Dali's nudes were a bit on the heavy side. This is a purely aesthetic observation. If I were painting a nude, I would make her slimmer and more elfin. Like Sky. Just an example, artistically speaking.

I got the book out of the library and showed Pete as we went off to RE. He was impressed. (With the book, not RE.)

'That is weird,' muttered Pete. 'That person's head looks like an egg that's cracking open.'

'It is an egg, but it's also a head,' I said.

'He must have been off his trolley,' Pete observed. 'Wow! Will you look at her!'

'That's his wife, Gala. He painted her loads. Hi, Delfine.'

She came running up from behind. 'Gross,' she said, looking at the nude. 'You're such a perv, Pete.'

'Not me. Stuff got it from the library.'

I shut the book and showed Delfine the cover. 'Salvador Dali, artist,' I read out.

'Perv, more like,' said Delfine.

'Me or him?'

'Both of you.'

'Why?'

'You don't see pictures of naked men like that, do you?'

'So, what are you saying? If it's a naked man, it's OK; if it's a naked woman, it's not?'

'Well, if it *was* a naked man I wouldn't stare like you two.'

'We weren't staring. We were looking. And we were looking at the other pictures too, like this one.'

'That's stupid,' said Delfine. 'Trains don't come out of fireplaces.'

I never thought I'd be pleased to reach an RE class. I made sure I sat next to Pete, even if he was a perv. I felt rotten. My relationship with Delfine was crumbling. I wanted it to happen and I didn't

33

want it to happen. I liked her. We'd been going out for ages—at least a month.

I slumped back in my seat and got ready to switch off RE. I hated it. It was actually RE and philosophy. We had Mrs Tightsparrow—yes, I know but, believe me, it really was her name—and she was one of the dreariest teachers in the school. I don't think she would have come alive if we'd plugged her into the mains. So you can guess how excited we were to be sitting there.

Then the door opens and in comes, not Mrs Tightsparrow, but a legend. I'd seen Mr Hanson before, but I'd never been taught by him. He taught sixth formers mostly—philosophy, RE, all the stuff that makes you shudder, and exactly the same as Mrs Tightsparrow.

But that is why he's a legend. It was amazing how many people liked his lessons. Everyone thinks he's awesome, which is weird, because he wears corduroy trousers and bright-yellow socks. And he's got a beard, a big one. A really big one. Like a dead badger. In the looks department he must rank as the uncoolest person on the planet. So what's the big deal? I was about to find out. He put a battered brown briefcase on the desk and eyed us for a moment.

'Mrs Tightsparrow is indisposed today. She will be indisposed tomorrow,' he rumbled. 'She may be indisposed beyond then. We are at the mercy of the gods. This morning, ladies, gentlemen, we must make do without her as best we can. I am going to show you a video. I don't suppose you'll understand it, but I'm going to show it to you anyway.'

A ripple of laughter ran through the room. This

was Hanson's catchphrase. He was famous for introducing almost every lesson by saying: 'I don't suppose you'll understand, but I'm going to tell you anyway.' Hanson ignored our laughter and slipped the video into the VCR.

It was a documentary drama about creating the first English dictionary.

Yes! I know! Exciting! I almost plunged straight into a deep coma.

Glad I didn't.

So, we watch this documentary about how this guy, Dr Johnson, took years and years to write the first English dictionary. This is about 250 years ago. And I'm watching this but it's getting a bit boring. I'm starting to switch off and then it starts telling you other things about Dr Johnson's life, like he had a mistress. The film showed them together but they had all their clothes on and I thought, what a bummer! All that lace and layers of clothing! It'd take you half an hour just to find something interesting. Johnson and his mistress certainly couldn't find anything—not that they'd have showed us, anyway. They always leave out the really educational bits. There was just a lot of grunting and hunting. We had to use our imagination. (So I did.)

And then the film says the Doc was a bit of a wise guy, always ready with a snappy answer: 'A cucumber should be well sliced, and dressed with pepper and vinegar, and then thrown out, as good for nothing.' That gave me a giggle. I heard Pete snort too. I'd chuck out the broccoli too.

Another time, Johnson was being told about some smart-brain philosopher who was suggesting that most of the things we see in the world are just an illusion. Johnson thought that was totally stupid. He went up to a big stone boulder and started shouting, 'I refute it, thus!' And he kicked the boulder.

'I refute it, thus!' he shouted again, and he went on kicking and kicking the boulder to show that it couldn't possibly be an illusion because it was hurting his foot. Then he went hopping off. Mad! (Quite possibly hopping mad, ha ha.) It was really funny. Pete and I were in hysterics.

Afterwards, when we were leaving, I told Pete that maybe school was just an illusion. 'Don't worry. It's not really here at all,' I said.

He went to the side of the corridor and began kicking the wall. 'I refute it, thus!' he shouted. 'Ow!'

At that moment old Hanson went past. His eyes slid sideways towards Pete. 'There is hope for the future,' he murmured.

God knows what he was on about.

Anyhow, it was brilliant. Pete and I spent the rest of the day refuting everything. At lunchtime one of the dinner ladies offered Pete some globulous goo she claimed was mashed potato.

'I refute it, thus!' said Pete, looking outraged, horrified and disgusted all in one go. And he plunged a fork right into the middle.

We were like that all afternoon. Nobody else had a clue what we were on about. Hilarious!

## RUNNING AWAY—FIRST ATTEMPT

Anyway, all this time I had been hatching my cunning plan for the Great Escape. The 'plan' bit of the Great Escape went like this: go and live with Pete and his Aunt Polly. The 'cunning' bit of the Great Escape was: do it when Dad isn't looking.

If you're going to run off somewhere, there's a lot to think about, even if you're only going as far as Pete's. For a start, you have to pack your bag. That was hard. Couldn't make up my mind about what I should put in and what I should leave out.

I'd run away once before, when I was five. Even then Mum and Dad were quarrelling with each other and it seemed like I was getting in the way, so I thought I'd remove myself from the scene and everything would be all right again. Tra la la.

**My Running-away Story**
I knew I couldn't just go. I would need something to eat, so I made a cheese sandwich. I'd never made one before but I'd seen Mum do it. The bread was already sliced, but cutting the cheese was difficult. I had to use two hands on the knife handle and every time I pressed down the slab of cheese shot off sideways somewhere. That cheese must have paid flying visits to every corner of the kitchen except the ceiling. It landed in the washing-up bowl at one point.

Anyhow, I eventually managed to produce

three or four tiny nicks of cheddar. I made the sandwich, stuck it in my jacket pocket and set off. I knew exactly where I was going and headed down the road. By the time I reached the corner I reckoned it was lunchtime, so I ate the sandwich. It didn't taste very cheesy but it did taste of washing-up liquid. Then I went round the corner and down to where my aunt and uncle lived.

I rang the doorbell and my aunt answered and she asked me what I was doing there.

'I'm running away from home,' I told her.

'Oh,' she said. 'You'd better come in, then. Does your mum know?'

'No. You're not supposed to tell your mum if you're running away,' I explained.

'Oh,' she said again.

My aunt gave me a drink and some chocolate biscuits. 'You eat those while I make a quick phone call,' she told me, and went out of the room.

When she came back we both sat there for a bit and she asked me what I wanted for my birthday and then there was a knock at the door and it was my mum.

'Hello, Simon,' she said with a big smile, giving me a hug. 'Those look like nice biscuits. Can I have one?'

'Yes.'

'We've been talking about Simon's birthday,' said my aunt, and we talked about it a bit more. Apparently I was going to have a party. I'd never had a party before. I'd been to two or three, but I'd never had one of my own and we sat there and talked about all the different

38

kinds of food I'd have and who I'd invite and, even more important, who I wouldn't invite.

'Not Roger Matthews,' I said, shaking my head. 'His dad's a librarian.'

My mum and aunt burst out laughing.

'Why is that so bad?' my mum asked.

I didn't like the way they laughed at me. I was serious, but I couldn't tell them why. The thing was, I'd been in the library a few weeks earlier and I'd been looking at a book and I was turning a page and there were two stuck together, so I tried to peel them apart and they both tore and pulled bits of the page surface off each other. The book was ruined. I looked around and nobody had seen, so I quickly shut the book and put it back in the box. The librarians must have found it by now and I reckoned they'd be furious. If they knew it was me, I'd be in dead trouble, so I had to keep away from anything to do with the library for as long as possible.

Listen, I was five at the time: bet you were stupid when you were five.

We sat there for half an hour or so talking about birthdays and parties and then Mum got up and said, 'Oh look, it's lunchtime. We'd better get back home, Simon.'

She took my hand and we walked home and we had lunch. Cheese sandwiches. With real cheese and no washing-up liquid. Mum never said anything about my running away. I've always wondered if she knew. Oh yeah, I needn't have worried about Roger Matthews anyhow, because he got chickenpox and couldn't come. The party was brilliant. I got

39

loads of prezzies, but all Roger got was spots.
**The End**

However, this time it was going to be the real thing and it would need meticulous planning, like a military operation.

* PHASE ONE: Pack two shirts, two pairs trousers, two pairs underpants, two pairs socks, two Ts, two pairs trainers, all my minidiscs and stuff to go with it, Buffy poster, copy of *Men Only* mag I'd 'borrowed' from Dad's collection that he thought I knew nothing about, money, toothbrush, toothpaste.

* PHASE Two: Leave note for Dad, saying I was OK and not to worry.

* PHASE THREE: Leave home when nobody else was around and make way to Pete's.

* PHASE FOUR: Freedom at Pete's. Hurrah! (With wild parties and stuff . . . !)

I couldn't wait.

## 9

## REFUTING MR TEDDY

I was halfway through Phase One when Natasha burst into my bedroom, just as I was peeling Buffy off the wall. It so happens that there is a notice on the front of my door that says:

## DO NOT ENTER WITHOUT KNOCKING.

And beneath that I had added:

### *Natasha—don't even bother!*

'Can't you read?' I asked her.
    'Yeah—it says don't bother knocking, just come right in.'
    'As if. You don't know what I might have been doing.'
    'You'll go blind,' she said.
    'You are so disgusting.'
    '*I'm* disgusting?!' Tasha's face puckered. 'Anyhow, have you got a bin liner?'
    'What for?'
    'That spot's bigger than your nose. If it gets any worse, we'll have to call in the Hazardous Chemical Unit. I could lance it for you, if you like. I'll get a skewer. And a bucket. Or the vacuum cleaner—that could suck it dry.'
    'Ha ha.' How I hated her! I hated her for coming into my room despite the warning. I hated her for making blood rush to my face in the way it

was right then. And I hated her because she knew it was all because of her and she thought she'd won. That was a lot of hate. 'What do you want, anyway?'

'Oh, nothing. Just that Mum says to remind you it's your week to do the washing-up.'

'Thank you for the reminder,' I said icily. 'That was just so important.'

Tasha smiled and went to the door. She turned back for a moment. 'Nice teddy' she said, and then she was gone.

Damn and blast and double triple quadruple damn squared with knobs on and sharp things that fly off and stick into lousy horrible stinking clever-arse girls!

I could hear her laughing outside my door, stuffing a hand over her mouth to stifle it. I could have kicked myself. Mr Teddy was right there, on my window sill. I'd forgotten all about him, never bothered to throw him away because . . .

. . . because . . .

. . . well . . .

. . . because . . . *I couldn't.*

All right? I couldn't do it. Mr Teddy had been with me forever. When I was a teething toddler I'd chewed his left ear until it was a ragged stump. We'd been through a lot together. I had taught him how to swim in the frog pond. He didn't like it very much and seemed to prefer getting waterlogged and sinking to the bottom. I even taught him to fly. I got an inner tube from my bike, nailed it to the window frame and catapulted him out. He went as far as next door's garden. I think if he'd flapped he'd have gone even further. And I buried him once. I wanted to know what it felt like to stand

42

beside a grave, crying, like they showed on telly sometimes. So I buried Mr Teddy and stood there and I didn't feel like crying at all, so I dug him up and went indoors, wondering what all the fuss was about.

So, it was Mr Teddy's furry ears (or rather his *one* remaining furry ear) that held most of my secrets. (Some secrets can't be told to anyone, not even teddies.) And then, when I had almost decided that I was too grown-up to keep him any longer, Mum and Dad said they were splitting. I couldn't lose Mr Teddy as well. I pushed him to the far corner of the window sill and that was where he was when Tasha spotted him, sitting in wise silence.

I yanked the door open. Tasha was already at the corner of the stairs. I hurled Mr Teddy after her.

'I refute him, thus!' I yelled.

Mr Teddy went cart-wheeling through the air, like one of those steel karate triple-prongy things. *Fwwitt-fwwitt-fwwitt-fwwitt.* Tasha turned the corner without even bothering to look back. At the same moment, La Trifle turned the corner coming *up* the stairs. Mr Teddy hurtled towards his target. *Fwwitt-fwwittt-fwwitt—SPLAMMM*! Just like a computer game. I almost expected to see La Trifle dissolve in a series of dots and vanish entirely. Unfortunately, she didn't. She did the other thing that computer monsters do and grew to twice her size, powered up by anger.

'How dare you!' bellowed Roaring Sherry Trifle Monster.

What could I do? I was defenceless. She picked up Mr Teddy and threw him back at me. What a

43

crap throw! Pathetic. Still, she had more dangerous weapons in her armoury. We faced each other on the landing, Trifle Monster's bosom heaving. Holy juggabumps! I thought there'd be a spillage. More work for the Hazardous Chemical Unit.

'What do you think you're doing?'

'I was refuting him,' I said meekly.

YOU'LL BACK ME UP, WON'T YOU? THIS WAS THE HONEST TRUTH!

At least she was stunned into silence for a moment. 'I beg your pardon?'

'I was refuting him.'

'I have no idea what you are going on about. You threw that thing at me.'

'Actually, I threw it at Tasha.'

'That's just as bad! I'm telling your father about this.'

Nothing new there, then. How my life goes.

## 10

## RUNNING AWAY—SECOND ATTEMPT

As you can imagine, I was in trouble. I tried to explain, but Dad waved a hand at me and said he was fed up with my protests: 'Nobody knows what you're talking about, Simon. Refuting teddies? It's gibberish. Tracey and Natasha and I are starting a new life together. You can't change that by throwing your teddy at us. It's time you grew up.'

La Trifle and her witch-daughter were standing behind him, smirking at me. It was three against one. Well, that's not fair, is it? Didn't seem to be much point in hanging around. I thought longingly of Pete's place. It was definitely time to go. I waited until things had settled down a bit, grabbed my bag, crept downstairs, went out the back door and I was off.

I can tell you, my heart was beating at some rate. I tried to stay calm and walk at normal speed, but with every step I took away from home my spirits lifted. It wasn't just the Great Escape, it was the movie *The Great Escape*, and by the time I reached Pete's place I was walking on air. I felt like every one of those prisoners in the film. (All the ones that didn't get shot, that is.) I sauntered up the path and rang the bell.

Pete answered. 'Hi, Stuff. How's tricks?'

'I've done it.' I gave him a proud grin.

'What? You sly gink!'

All I could do was nod. I thought that if I grinned much more my mouth would split my face in half. Pete was gobwalloped. 'How did you do it? What did you say to her?'

The grin turned to puzzlement. 'How do you mean? What did I say to who?'

'Sky,' answered Pete. 'What did you say? How did you pull her?'

'I'm not talking about Sky,' I explained.

'You're not?'

'No.' Why was I disappointed at that look of relief on Pete's face?

'What are you talking about, then?'

A woman appeared from behind Pete and peered over his shoulder. It was Aunt Polly. We'd met before, once or twice, but only briefly. She was one of those glamorous aunts—the sort that your

45

friends have, but you never do—you know, the kind of woman that just looks . . . young, sexy, attractive, adventurous. She was the sort of woman you dreamed about meeting on the Orient Express at night and the train goes round a sharp bend and you stumble against the door to her compartment and it opens by mistake and you crash inside and go sprawling across her and she's in bed and it all gets interesting. Then you wake up and change your shorts. Crashed the Citroen again.

Sorry, got a bit carried away, but you know what I mean. It happens. Maybe I should explain about the Citroen. Maybe I shouldn't. But I'm going to. We had a sex-ed lesson a few months back and our biology teacher explained the mechanics of a stiffy. 'It's basically the same principle that Citroens use for hydropneumatic suspension,' he told us. You can work the rest out yourself. Pete and I can't see a Citroen without laughing now.

Anyhow, Pete's aunt wasn't laughing and she didn't look all that glamorous either. She stood in front of him, looking at me questioningly.

'Stuff?' (She never called me Simon. She was the only adult I knew who called me Stuff. I suppose it was because that was what Pete called me most of the time.)

'Hi.'

'What do you want?'

I smiled and tugged on my bag strap. 'Pete and I were talking the other day and I was telling him about how things are at my house.'

Pete was gesticulating at me from behind his aunt. He looked as if he was trying to cut his throat. He'd make his eyes big and then go cross-eyed. What was that supposed to mean?

46

'Yes? So?' Aunt Polly raised her eyebrows questioningly.

'Yeah, and Pete said . . .'

Pete was jumping up and down behind her and mouthing something at me. I couldn't make out what it was. His aunt caught me staring at him and swung round to see what was going on. He immediately stopped and pretended he was smoothing his hair and when she turned back he started all over again, pulling stupid faces.

'And Pete said it would be OK for me to stay here.'

At which point Pete's tongue came right out, his eyes rolled up, his head fell to one side and stayed there. Evidently he was dead.

'Pete was wrong,' said Aunt Polly. 'You can't.'

'Oh.' I looked at Pete, but he was still dead. I took a step back from the front door. 'I'll go home, then,' I said.

'Good idea,' said Aunt Polly, and her last bit of glamour faded away. 'Goodbye.'

I gave a little nod and set off back home. And, funnily enough, it took me all the way back to when I was five. I felt the same then: a strange mix of disappointment and relief. I hadn't made it but, on the other hand, I was going back to what I knew best. Not knowing what's in store for you can be a bit nerve-racking.

When I got home I hurried up to my room. I was putting Buffy back on the wall when my mobile went.

'I tried to warn you,' Pete said.

'Yeah. I worked that out—afterwards. You said it would be OK. I felt such a gobbersaurus.'

'That's because you are a gobbersaurus.

47

Couldn't you see what I was trying to say?'

'If I had, I wouldn't have made such a fool of myself, would I?'

'She's bust up with toy boy. He told her she was too old for him. She's spitting mad. She's making my life a misery now. You think you've got problems? I tell you, Stuff, if you're going to leg it, I reckon I should come with you.'

'Yeah?

'Yeah.'

'Serious?'

'Serious.'

'Deal?'

'Deal.'

I killed the phone, lay back on my bed and grinned madly at the ceiling. Result!

11

SHOCK! HORROR!

When the *Titanic* sank, more than 500 kilograms of marmalade went down with her. As if drowning the sausages wasn't enough. Five hundred kilograms! That's well over 1,000 jars. What a waste. I like marmalade. And sausages.

But, and here's a question, have you ever wondered how things like marmalade were invented? I mean, what kind of person goes around thinking, *I know what I'm going to do this morning: I'm going to get some oranges, peel them, stew them, slice the peel and pop that in, add some sugar, shove it in jars and call it marmalade?* I mean, somebody had to think of that.

And another thing. Why did they call it *marmalade?* What made them shove it in a jar, stare at it and announce, 'Behold, I have made a Thing to Eat, and it is a Good Thing, and it shall be called Marmalade for all Time, from Now until Eternity.'

Why didn't they just say, 'Oh, look, I've made some jollopy orange stuff.'

Anyhow, jollopy orange stuff—I like it. Small comforts are often the most important, so marmalade was near the top of my list of What I Need To Take With Me When I Go.

And I am going. Definitely. If yesterday wasn't the last straw, then today was. Dad and Sherry Trifle called a Family Conference. Family? Ha! A dad with a son, a mum with a daughter, but the mum and the dad aren't married to each other but to other people, and the son and the daughter aren't brother and sister. Some family.

There we are, all four of us sitting at the dining table, and Dad's looking at La Trifle du Jour and she's smiling and looking at him and they're holding hands across the table—urr, finger-downthroat. Tasha's giving me the Evil Eye, which is actually normal for her, and Pankhurst is out in the kitchen honing her claws on the knife sharpener.

So, we're round this table and there are lightning bolts of hate zagging between Tasha and me, while puddles of love ooze across the table between Dad and La Trifle. Neither of them notices, of course. Too busy squelching in the puddles.

'Tracey and I want to tell you something,' said

Dad, smiling broadly at everyone.

*Oh my God, they're going to get married.*

'It might come as a bit of a shock.'

*Budgie's buttocks! They want me to be a bridesmaid.'*

'Tracey's expecting a baby.'

!!!!!

'Say something, then.'

'Congratulations, Mum,' said Tasha, with an unusually bright smile.

'Thank you, darling. Simon?'

'Interesting,' was all I could manage, in a kind of *I'm being crushed by six pythons* voice.

'Interesting?' queried Dad.

I nodded and got up. 'I need some time to think about it.'

'That's fine,' said La Trifle coldly. 'You've got about eight months to get used to it.'

I went to my room, shut the door and died.

I lay on my bed and stayed dead for about an hour, I guess. A baby, a little half-brother or half-sister for our half-family. Dad and La Trifle were starting again, making their own family. Evidently Natasha thought it was wonderful. I didn't.

Dad knocked and came in. He looked sheepish. Baaaa. I turned to the wall.

'It came as a shock to me too,' he said.

'Really? Do you want me to tell you where babies come from?'

'Simon!'

'It's OK, Dad,' I grunted. 'I'll get used to it.'

And he left. But I won't get used to it and I was thinking that I had no option but to leave and start again, somewhere else. Seemed like nothing was

50

going for me at all—except, strangely enough, the comic strip. According to Secret Agent Kovak, it was going down a storm. Apparently the kids couldn't get enough of it, including the sixth formers! She'd even seen it in the staffroom. Mr Hanson reckoned it was the best thing the school had produced. 'It's honest,' he told her. 'I've always known rabbits were full of evil intent.'

So that made me feel better inside. Just a pity it didn't make me feel better enough. I went to see Pete.

'Is your aunt in?' I asked.

He grinned. 'No. Got a new boyfriend.'

'That was quick. How does she do it?'

'She just asks them, straight out. She doesn't hang about, my aunt. She says, "Time waits for no man and I'm not waiting for a man either. If you want one you have to go out and get one." Her words, not mine.'

'What do you do if you want a woman, not a man?'

Pete gave me a quick glance. 'Anyone in particular?'

'No.'

What a great big whoppa-doppa. Mind you, it was hardly likely that I was going to tell Pete about Sky. That's who I was thinking of. Most of the time. But I didn't think I had any chance of getting anywhere with her and a tiny bit of me kept muttering: Stick with Delfine. You know where you are with Delfine.

That was half the problem. I knew only too well where I was with Delfine. Going nowhere. The last time we'd been out together I'd tried kissing her in a special way. I'd read it in a book. OK, it was a

51

girlie book. Tasha had left it lying around and every time I'd seen her reading it she was laughing. I wondered what was so funny about it and, when she wasn't looking, I picked it up and read a bit.

It was all about lip-nibbling. Apparently girls like it if you nibble their lips. They do! Apparently—according to this book. I thought I'd try it with Delfine. She leaped away from me as if I'd just bitten her. (Well, I had, sort of.)

'What are you *doing?!*'

'Lip-nibbling.'

'It's horrid!'

'It's supposed to be nice. You're supposed to like it.' I told her about the book.

'That's disgusting,' she said.

'It says girls like it in the book.'

'You shouldn't read things like that. You read too much. If you didn't read so much, you wouldn't be like you are.'

'How do you mean, "be like you are"? What am I, then?'

'Weird,' said Delfine, clamping her arms across her chest.

Long silence.

'Look,' I said, 'think of it as an experiment. If you don't try, you won't know what it's like. You'll never know if you like it or not. It's the same as ravioli.'

'What? What's ravioli?'

'It's a kind of pasta—you know, spaghetti, lasagne, macaroni? There are loads of different kinds of pasta. Penne—that's another one.'

'I don't like pasta,' Delfine said.

'I'm not giving you pasta! I'm asking you to use your imagination for a moment. Suppose you're in

52

a restaurant and the waiter comes up and asks if you'd like some ravioli?'

'That's pasta, isn't it? You said.'

'Yeah,' I nodded.

Delphine shook her head emphatically. 'Don't like it,' she said.

'How do you know? You've never tried ravioli.'

'It's pasta. Don't like pasta.'

Another long silence. Trying to argue sensibly with Delfine was like attempting to reach the centre of a maze that had no centre. I tried to give her a cuddle.

'Are you going to do that nibbling thing again?' she asked, backing off. She made it sound as if I was trying to remove all the fillings in her teeth with a blunt tablespoon.

'I think I'll go home,' I said. And I did.


12

## VERY USEFUL LISTS

So, there I was at Pete's, thinking about Sky. Couldn't stop thinking about her. Why not? OK, she was stunning. But that was purely coincidental. Purely. There was more to it than that.

So, when Pete asked if I had some particular girl in mind, I clammed up. I'd seen the way he looked at her. Pete and I were best mates, but he went through girls like, I dunno: a hurricane, boa constrictor, cocktail stick? Whatever. I knew he had his eye on Sky, so I thought it best to keep quiet for the time being. Apart from anything else,

I had no idea how to deal with Sky myself. So far there was nothing between us at all and no sign from Sky that she thought it might ever be any different. In fact, since that episode in the art room, she'd been positively cool with me. Maybe I'd embarrassed her so much she was avoiding me.

When Pete had told me what his aunt said about not hanging around—you know, just go out and make it happen—I thought that's what I should do.

I should go to Sky and say: 'Will you go out with me?' It was the only way to find out. Simple.

On the other hand (and it was a giant hand, so to speak), the whole business had just been cocked up by Dad and the Pregnant Trifle. I spilled the beans to Pete.

'It's going to be awful.'

Pete sat on his bed, nodding. 'Yeah. How's that?'

'A *baby,* Pete. Not even my brother or sister—only half.'

'Hey, I've got an idea. You wait until the baby is born, then you stand over the cot and point at the baby very severely and you say the magic words.'

'What magic words?'

'You point VERY severely and you say, "I refute you, thus!" Then throw the cot out of the window.'

'Pete!'

'Only trying to help. It's like the cucumber. You could put salt and pepper on the baby first, if you wanted.'

'Pete! This is serious. I feel like I've been snatched from my real family and found myself being fostered by strangers. I've got to get out. Are you serious about coming with me?'

'What? Oh yeah. Too right, I am.'

'I thought maybe things were better with your aunt now she has a new boyfriend.'

'They are, but you never know how long it'll last. She's up and down all the time. I never know what to expect. You know what women are like.'

I smiled and nodded but I was thinking: *No, I don't know what women are like at all. I really wish I did. I'd love to know what women are like. Well, girls, at any rate. Especially Sky.* And I wished I was Pete. He knew so much. He had so much experience. Sometimes I felt like a ten-year-old when I was with him.

'OK, if we're going to go away, we need a plan and we need to think about what to take with us.'

'Money,' said Pete.

'Make a list,' I suggested, so he swung round to the processor and began work.

ESSENTIALS
* Loads of dosh
* Clothes, shoes, jacket
* Rope, crampons, ice axe (Pete reckoned we might head for Scotland)
* Matches, batteries, multi-tool knife, cooking gear, pans, plates

These last items got us thinking about the sort of things we might cook.

'Scrambled eggs is easy,' Pete said. 'And sausages. Fried bread, eggy-bread, fried egg, baked beans, bacon—they're all easy. I've had to do those when Aunt Polly's been out.'

This was typical Pete—a man of the world. I was feeling ten again. The only thing I could think of was cheese on toast, which happened to be one of my favourites. (Cheese on toast *and* marmalade *and* sausages—but not all at once.)

Pete shook his head. 'Don't know the recipe.'

'It's easy. Get a slice of bread. Get a slice of cheese. Toast bread. Put cheese on top and there you are—cheese on toast.'

'Can't do toast,' said Pete. 'We won't have a toaster.'

This was a blow—all that way from home and no cheese on toast. But I saw Pete's point. We could hardly take a pop-up toaster with us. We'd need miles of electric cable. Then I remembered that you could get wind-up radios. You didn't have to plug them in anywhere. You wound them up with a handle to generate their own electricity.

'Maybe we could make a wind-up toaster?' I suggested.

'OK,' said Pete, and he added it to the list. 'Beds would be nice too, especially our own beds.'

'Put them on the list,' I grinned, and after that we just got silly.

* Wind-up toaster
* Our own beds, duvets, pillows
* Toilet on wheels; in fact, why not the whole house?
* Rest of road, except Mrs Parkinson and her horrible dog
* Aunt Polly's car
* Sky

'You can't take Sky!' I protested.
  'Why not?'
  'She wouldn't go with you.'
  'I'll ask. Time waits for no woman.'

56

'Dare you!'

'No probs.'

We eyed each other. Did Pete know what I was thinking? Did I know what Pete was thinking? Did Pete know I thought I knew what he was thinking? Confused? So was I.

When I got back home Tasha and Pankhurst were prancing round the room to Honzo da Bonzo yet again—not a pretty sight, or sound for that matter. I was going to walk straight past and up the stairs but I was surprised (and annoyed) to see that Tasha was a good dancer, sexy even. (Pankhurst was crap.) Tasha had her eyes closed, dancing in a world of her own. *If only she'd go and live there,* I thought. Anyhow, she wasn't aware I'd seen her. I went upstairs before she found out.

I sat on my bed and began my own list. A proper list. A serious one.

* Tins of food, cutlery, scissors
* Pots, pans, plates
* Buttons, needles, thread
* Torch, candles, matches, batteries
* First-aid kit, string, torch
* Fishing line and hooks, sharp knife
* Compass, mirror, magnifying glass, map

I studied my list for a while. I thought about Delfine, Natasha, La Trifle and new babies. I thought about Mum, in another town up north with a new man and a new life. I wondered if she'd have a baby. That would make another family I only half belonged to, another half-brother or half-sister.

I added two more items:

* Marmalade
* Sky




13

## HOW TO EMBARRASS YOURSELF

Hail to the King! Miss Kovak thinks I'm a genius. Quite right too. Apparently she had to print off extra copies of *Art Works,* but only the comic-strip bit.

'The teachers were asking for copies,' she said. 'They thought it was funny and well drawn.'

'Did anyone recognize themselves?'

'Apart from Sky, who's a bit obvious, no, but I think some of the staff reckoned they spotted likenesses.'

'Am I in trouble?' I was already worrying about Baguette.

'No! And I can't wait for the next instalment.'

That gave me something to think about. I was beginning to get a good idea of what shape it would take. I remembered what Miss Kovak had said about drawing what was in the world I knew— the world of home and school. There were things going on around me all the time that I could use.

It's a strange business, sketching. When you draw something you really focus on it and you start seeing things you've never noticed before. Take your eye, for example. Obviously I don't mean that literally. Leave it in its socket for the time being. Use a mirror, you gormless goat. But look at that

58

eye. Do you see how many little flecks of colour make up your iris? Tiny shards of gold, white, carmine, green . . . see what I mean?

Anyhow, I was pretty chuffed that the first episode had been successful. I was dying to tell everyone about it—Pete, Delfine, even Dad—but I couldn't. It had to be a secret. Have you ever had a secret you couldn't tell? What a stupid question. That's exactly what a secret is. But have you? I had this really embarrassing secret when I was younger.

## My Second Most Embarrassing Experience

When I was ten I had a girlfriend at school called Molly. In the summer she went away on holiday with her family and I was lonely. I was hoping to get a postcard from her, but she never sent one. So in the end I had to write one myself, to myself. I got a piece of paper and wrote this letter:

---

Dear Simon

It is hot here. The weather is good.
I wish you were here.
I love you so much. You are wonderful.
I can't live without you.
I think you are so clever and strong. You have nice hair.
I want to marry you and kiss you forever.
Lots and lots and lots of love,
Molly

x x x x x x x x x x x
x x x x x x x x x x

---

I put it under my pillow and every night I read it before I went to sleep and I felt a lot better. But then my mum found it and I didn't know. So what happened next was, Molly and her parents came back from their holiday and my mum took the letter round to their house and said, 'Look what your depraved daughter has been writing to my son. Goodness me! She's ten years old—wicked girl!'

Only, of course, she hadn't and she wasn't. Weren't they surprised! Yes, of course they were. So they sent for me and asked me what I knew about the letter and I wanted the ground to swallow me up, but it didn't and instead I had to stand there and admit that it was me.

Were they cross?

No. Instead they shrieked and roared with laughter. All except for Molly and me. Molly cried and I wanted to die. She never spoke to me again.

**End of Second Most
Embarrassing Experience**

Which is just as well, because otherwise I would now have three women to juggle instead of two. And if you want to know what my first most embarrassing moment was, I might tell you later.

But I was really pleased about my drawings and I was looking forward to doing some more because, like I said, I was getting one or two ideas. Most important of all, though, it would mean drawing Sky.

14

DARCY

**A Short Note About Cuckoos**
I don't know how much you know about
cuckoos, so I shall assume you know nothing
and start from scratch. If you do know
something, then you can skip this little bit if you
want. (Off you go, skippity-skip.)
Cuckoos are as big as magpies. They don't
make nests for themselves but search around
for nests built by small little birdies. When they
find a suitable nest, they lay their egg in it.
Then they fly away. That's it. That's their bit of
parenting done. (I know some people like that)
So, there's the cuckoo egg, in a nest belonging
to, let's say, a robin. The nest has four little
robin eggs and one whopping great cuckoo
egg in it. The robin doesn't appear to notice.
Big mistake. The eggs all hatch out—four
robins and one cuckoo. Of course, the cuckoo
is already bigger than the tiny, helpless, little
baby robins. The first thing the baby cuckoo
does is start pushing at the newborn robins.
The cuckoo pushes the little babby-boos up the
side of the nest, right up to the edge, over the
top and, whoops, oh dear, now they're
FALLING, FALLING, falling, and they haven't
got wings yet and they can't fly, so they fall and
fall until SPLAT, they hit the ground and they're
dead. End of baby robins. And the mummy and
daddy robin just carry on, feeding the cuckoo

because they think it's their little babby-child.

ARE THEY STUPID? CAN'T THEY SEE THEY'RE FEEDING A GIANT?

No, they can't. This is Nature's way of ensuring that there will always be cuckoos.

It's tough out there. How life goes.

**End of Cuckoo Bit**

You will find out later why I have told you the above. Now I am going to change the subject and horrify you with information about Delfine's stinknoid brother, Darcy.

Darcy is sixteen. He does a lot of bunking-off school and hanging around the town centre with his mates and matelles, or whatever you call female mates. I don't wish to give them the nice title of 'girlfriends' because when they're all together they look and behave more like a pack of hunting baboons, whooping around the precinct.

You are probably reading this and thinking that Darcy sounds like a right yobbo.

You are so wrong. It's more scary than that.

When you first meet Darcy you are impressed, because Darcy is tall and even handsome, if you like that sort of look. He's well spoken. In fact, adults are impressed with his good manners and politeness. But what the adults don't experience is Darcy's vicious sadism. Basically, he's a bully—the quiet kind. He speaks softly, lulling you into a sense of security and then, all of a sudden, he lashes out—fist, arm, leg, foot, head, doesn't really matter which. Because from then on all you feel is PAIN.

Darcy goes to the gym for bodybuilding. He

does judo and tae kwon do. He does boxing. In fact, he does a lot of stuff that involves hitting things. He likes hitting things.

This may lead you to the conclusion that what Darcy really needs is LOVE and AFFECTION. LOVE will soothe his fevered brain and melt his anger. Come here, Darcy, and let us spread LOVE's calming balm around you. After all, something must have made him the way he is. Don't ask me what.

Well, I think what Darcy really needs is to be spread with honey and shut inside an ants' nest. Really BIG ants. Really BIG nest. Nibble nip ow.

Imagine my utter delight when I saw Delfine at school and she said: 'My brother wants to see you.' That brightened my day! Bee's buttocks! She might just as well have handed me a note saying: *YOU WILL BE SHOT AT LUNCHTIME, VERY SLOWLY; WITH BLUNT BULLETS.*

'What have you been saying to him now?' I asked.

'Nothing. He saw me crying.'

'Why were you crying?'

'Because of you.'

'What did I do?'

'You like Sky. I know you do.'

'We've hardly spoken to each other!'

'Everybody knows. Everyone knows about it.'

'Knows about what?'

'You drew her.'

This rather knocked the breath from me. What did Delfine know? For a second or two I almost panicked. Then I remembered that stupid conversation I'd had with Pete when he reckoned I must have drawn Sky in the nuddy. I bet he'd been

63

winding Delfine up. It was just the sort of thing he'd do. And look where it had landed me. Thanks, Pete.

'It was our art lesson. We all had to draw a portrait of someone else.'

'She was almost naked.'

(Yep, that was Pete all right! If only it were true!) 'That's news to me.'

'You know what I mean. You drew her all . . . thingy.'

Obviously *thingy* was something so awful Delfine couldn't even think of the proper word, let alone say it.

'I drew her, that's all.'

'You've never drawn me.'

'Delfy, you're not in my art class.'

'Darcy says he'll see you at lunchtime.' She stared at the ground for a moment, sniffed and then walked off.

It was a wee bit difficult to concentrate on school after that. Lunchtime arrived and so did Darcy, looking cool, casual and, therefore, at his most dangerous. He glanced around to make sure the corridor was clear, then shoved me back against a wall.

'You've been giving my little sister the runaround.'

'No.'

'Oh yes, dear boy, I think you have.'

'I haven't.'

'Never argue with Darcy, you mucoid wozzer. That's not the way to sort things out.'

'I'm trying to explain . . . Ow!'

My head thudded back against the wall as Darcy pushed me again.

'I know all about your dirty little drawings, you pustulous puss-pot. You'd better listen to me very carefully. Are your ears pinned back, ready to listen? Do let me assist.'

'Ow!'

'Now my little fuzzbag, you be good to Delfine or you'll feel this.' Darcy waved a fist in my face. 'Upset her one more time and you'll be history.'

'Right,' I choked.

Darcy took a step back and reached into his pocket. 'And I have a little task for you. Make sure your sister gets this, or you'll have to answer to me and I don't think you'll want to do that, dear boy.' He smiled and stuffed a piece of paper in my shirt pocket.

'She's not my—' but he was already striding off—'sister,' I finished weakly, gazing after him. What on earth did he want with Natasha?

I pulled the note from my shirt and opened it up. It was scribbled in pencil, with several mistakes.

**To my smasher,
Nattasher.
I lik you. You
look god. Cum out with me.
Darcy xxxxxxxx**

Hell in a thing-thong! Tasha was a god! Darcy wanted to lick her! (Urgh!) A love letter! What a laugh!

## 15

## THE GRANGE
## (CREEPY STUFF)

On the other hand, maybe not such a laugh after all. Darcy fancied my stepsister. *Serves her right,* I thought. They suited each other. Mind you, it was the sort of thing you wouldn't wish on your worst enemy, and Tasha just about was my worst enemy. So, should I give her the note and cause a lot of grief for her, or pretend to lose the note and cause a lot of grief for myself? It was grief either way, courtesy of Darcy Smith.

What I couldn't understand was why he wrote like that—all those mistakes. It was obviously deliberate, but why? Was he trying to disguise himself in some way? He'd signed the letter with his own name, so it couldn't be that. Was it a joke? That could be it. His sense of humour was loopy enough.

Have you ever noticed how just one person can cause so much misery? Darcy was spreading doom and gloom around the school like poison gas. Now he wanted to get Tasha into his clutches.

I didn't see Tasha until school had long finished and I got home. I pulled out the crumpled note. 'I was asked by the writer of this to pass it on to you.'

Tasha read it and blanched. 'Oh my God,' she

murmured. 'He's a sadist.'

Wonder of wonders—Tasha and I actually agreed with each other about something, not that I was going to let on.

'I'm not going out with him,' she said.

'Fine. Tell him.'

Tasha shook her head. 'You tell him. You brought the note. You can take one back.'

'What? He'll kill me!'

'Don't be stupid.'

'He's a maniac.'

Tasha ignored me, got a piece of paper and began writing. It didn't take long. She passed the note across.

> Dear Darcy,
> Sorry—I don't go out with moronic baboons who can't even spell my name properly.
> Never yours, Natasha.

I looked at her. 'You're really serious about getting me killed, aren't you?'

'Don't be so dramatic. Darcy won't kill you.' Tasha paused and gave a little smile. 'He might rearrange you slightly, I suppose, but look on the bright side.'

'Which is . . . ?'

'You can see the hospital from the school.' Another pause while she listened to the sound of me not laughing. 'Look, he won't touch you. This is between me and him. Just give him the note and tell him exactly that—it's between him and me.

You are not responsible.'

I took the note and went up to my room to take stock. What sort of state was my world in now? Well, Tasha was making my life miserable, Darcy was about to turn me into a very good copy of a pile of mashed potato, Delfine seemed to think I was some kind of sex maniac, La Trifle was going to produce a cuckoo for the nest, and Sky wasn't speaking to me.

*Definitely time to go,* I thought. (You see? I was already being pushed by that cuckoo.)

I slipped downstairs to the kitchen, snitched a frying pan and a tin-opener and hid them under my bed. I'd find a better place later. I needed to get them out of the house and somewhere safe where I could pick them up when I was ready to go. But where? That was when I remembered The Grange.

The Grange was like something out of a horror movie. It had once been lived in by triplets—three elderly sisters. They had been born there, all within an hour of each other, and they had died there eighty-seven years later, all within an hour of each other. Spooky or what? The house had been empty ever since. Ivy had crept up the walls and through the windows. So had spiders. There were rumours that the spiders inside The Grange had grown bigger than elephants, but that might have been someone exaggerating—quite possibly me. It was a place full of ghosts and memories, cobwebs and strange shadows. It had such a feeling of doom, death and despondency that people kept well clear.

It would be the ideal hiding place. I shoved the bits and pieces I had scrounged so far into a

68

rucksack, slipped from the house and went straight there.

Creepy? Oh yes. The back door was so rotten I hardly had to look at the lock before it fell off. The smell was like being inside the tomb of an ancient pharaoh—not that I've ever been inside one, but I bet it would smell like The Grange. The floor was littered with bits of broken furniture, old newspapers, the odd photograph.

My heart was thudding. I kept expecting to see the circling fins of sharks as they closed in, ready to surge forward and take off both my legs.

Yes, I know, you don't get sharks in dining rooms; that's how creepy it was. It made you think daft, scary things. I tried to calm my nerves by searching for a safe place to stash my equipment. In one of the rooms I discovered an old piano, standing forlornly in the corner. There was something about the instrument that brought ghostly pictures to mind of the three sisters—one playing, one turning the pages of the music, one singing. I could almost see them. I could almost hear them. *Tra la la, liddle-lee, dee-lah . . .*

That was me, humming to myself in a squeaky, nervous voice. I pulled the piano forward a little way and stacked my kit behind it. Then I crept out, back to the garden, back to the road. I grinned to myself. I had made a proper start at last. Phew.

## 16

## DARCY AGAIN

Have you ever considered how much time you spend at school? Have you ever wondered why it is that teachers can retire, but us kids can't? What I say is: bring the age of retirement down to fourteen.

Anyhow, school—it dominates your life. In fact, if you think of Time as a mountain range, then school would be Mount Everest. Consider this: you arrive aged four and a half and you leave . . . let's say, at sixteen. That's eleven and a half years, and each year you spend forty-one weeks at school— that's two hundred and five days. Six hours a day— that's one thousand, two hundred and thirty hours a year and, all in all, fourteen thousand, one hundred and forty-five hours of your life. In other words, eight hundred and forty-eight thousand, seven hundred minutes. Or fifty million, nine hundred and twenty-two thousand seconds.

A whole Mount Everest of Time.

Anyway, there I was, back at Mount Everest and wondering when Death (alias Darcy) would show up. I was pacing the corridors, hoping I wouldn't bump into him, when I bumped straight into—Sky. Sent her sprawling. *Splat.*

I just stood there, staring down at her. I was horrified, embarrassed, stricken. I didn't know what to do. Should I help her up? If I touched her, what would she say? Would she scream? All this was going through my head in a flash.

Sky raised herself on one elbow and looked up at me. 'Are you all right?' she asked.

I swallowed and nodded, still speechless.

'Oh good,' she went on evenly. 'I'm glad. Now it's your turn.'

'Uh?'

'Now you say to me, "Are you all right? I'm sorry I just knocked you off your feet. I hope you didn't hurt yourself, falling on to that hard floor, Sky. You haven't broken anything, have you? Here, let me help you up."'

I must have looked brain-dead because she started to laugh as she clambered to her feet. 'You're weird,' she said.

'It's my genes,' I answered as my brain began to return to some form of normal function.

'You're not wearing jeans,' observed Sky.

'No, *genes,* as in DNA and stuff.'

'Right,' nodded Sky. 'How does that work, then? Why does your DNA make you bump into people and knock them over?'

'My mother was a bulldozer.' God! What was I saying? Now she'd think I was a complete gobbersaurus.

Sky smiled. She laughed. My heart went off like some million-starred exploding firework with whizz-bangs, doo-lallies and sparkly-sprinkles. It slowly reassembled itself. She looked so wonderful when she smiled. I felt myself grinning back at her like some love-struck teenager. I didn't care. I *was* a love-struck teenager!

'I love the strip,' she said. 'I know Miss Kovak said it's a secret, but since I know and you know, it's . . . you know!'

'Do you really like it?'

71

She nodded.

I swallowed hard. OK. Here goes. 'Would you go out with me?' I asked.

Sky's eyebrows shot up and she took a step back. 'Sorry,' she frowned. 'But I don't two-time.'

Damn! She already had a boyfriend. Hardly surprising, but bloody annoying. She smiled again but now she had her lips pressed together in that kind of oh-well-better-get-on-it's-a-rotten-life kind of way.

'Nice to bump into you,' she said, and off she went.

I watched her walk up the corridor, unable to take my eyes off her. I loved the way she walked. Hip talk. I loved everything about her.

'I told you he liked her.'

Delfine's voice brought me crashing back into the real world, a world that not only contained Delfine, but big brother Darcy too. He pushed me against the wall.

'I thought I told you to keep your hands off Sky, scuzzbag.'

'You did, I was. I mean, I have, I am, I will. We bumped into each other, that's all, and she fell over and—'

'You fancy her, I know you do! You were laughing with her.' Delfine pushed out her lower lip. It quivered. Very soap opera.

'I don't fancy her,' I lied, hoping it didn't show (Yep, I know it's not right to tell lies; it's not nice, but I was trying to SAVE MY LIFE.)

Darcy shoved me against the wall again, banging my head. He was making a habit of this and I didn't like it. Apart from anything else, I was worried because the more the wall hit the back of my head the more it felt as if the jolt was raising more and more acne spots.

'This is your last warning, dearest pustule,' he growled, twisting my tie until I could barely breathe. 'If I see you chatting up that girl again, I'm afraid that I shall have to rearrange all your teeth for you, one by one. Permanently. Understand?'

I nodded rapidly, unable to speak.

'Now, then, how is that other little matter with your rather gorgeous sister coming on?' He let go of my throat at last.

I coughed and gasped. 'Not my sister . . . stepsister.'

'My dear piece of slobbersnot, I don't care if she's your grandfather. What did she say?'

I pulled Tasha's note from my pocket and handed it over.

Darcy read it through, very slowly. 'What does that say?' he asked.

' "Moronic baboons",' I said miserably.

I could see the anger building up inside him. It was like watching air go into a tyre and you know it's certain to burst but you don't know exactly when and you don't know exactly where. Darcy read the letter over and over.

'What does it say?' Delfine asked.

'Doesn't matter,' muttered her brother. 'You'd better go to your class, Delfy. I'll see to your boyfriend.'

Darcy looked at me like he was calculating how many different ways he could find to kill me. He only needed one. All I felt was the blow. It was as unexpected as a steam train thundering out of a fireplace—a steam train wearing knuckledusters.

(Very big knuckledusters obviously, specially adapted for trains.) I collapsed in a heap. I couldn't scream. I couldn't cry. I had no breath left. I doubled up on the floor, holding myself, fighting for air. Darcy pinned me down with one foot on my side.

'I'm not an idiot,' he declared. 'Your sister would never have written this. You did it. Did you think you could get the better of me? I'm afraid not. You'll have to try a lot, lot harder. You give that letter I wrote to your sister.' Darcy bent down and put his mouth close to my face. 'I think it would be best if you do as I ask. You don't want to put your family in the gruesome position of trying to identify your mangled remains. I really don't know what my little sister sees in you. I really don't.'

He lifted his foot, but only so he could kick me.

17

## DECISION TIME

I lay there until I saw him turn the corner. I sat up, aching all over. This was crazy. I don't mind getting into trouble when I've done something wrong, but I was innocent! I wished Sky would come back along the corridor and find me slumped, injured, bleeding. She'd crouch down and cradle my head against her chest. *Hmmm, hold that thought,* I thought.

Pete says men think about sex every six seconds. That's OK by me, though it does make me wonder what we think about for the other five. Or if, in fact, we think for the other five seconds at all. Pete reckons he's special and says he thinks about it every four seconds.

'How do you know?' I asked.

'I counted.'

'Yeah, but all you'd have to do is look at your watch and make yourself think about it every four seconds.'

'Yeah, but I don't have to make myself—that's the point. I just do, naturally.'

'I could think about it every two seconds if I wanted.'

'Go on, then,' he challenged.

Ten seconds later. 'There. Told you.'

'How do I know what you were thinking? Prove it.'

'No. You prove you think about it every four seconds.'

Pete burst out laughing. 'Idiot! We've been talking about nothing else for the last three minutes!'

Anyhow, where was I? Oh yes, nestling against Sky's chest, my head against her . . . I can't say the word. You know. My heart's thumping. I tried touching Delfine there once. She asked me what I was doing.

'Touching you,' I said, because I was.

'Well, don't.'

So that was that. I had learned nothing. How was I supposed to grow up and expand my education if knowledge was denied me? But Sky wouldn't be like that. She'd stroke my hair and speak softly and say nice things and KISS ME BETTER! Oh yes. Best bit. I wonder if she'd like lip-nibbling? Maybe she'd read that book. Maybe I should ask again. Maybe she would go out with me. Shame about the boyfriend.

And here we go, back to square one, and Problemo Numero Uno. Delfine. I was coming to the inescapable conclusion that I would have to break up with Delfine. And, if I dumped Delfine, then Darcy the Destroyer would slaughter me.

Brainwave! Darcy was going to kill me anyway because he thought that note hadn't come from Tasha, and it had, so he was bound to take it out on me because I couldn't deliver it again. So, if Darcy was going to kill me for that, he couldn't kill me for dumping Delfine, because I'd already be dead. There—saved! Well, saved for my coffin at any rate. Maybe Sky would weep at my funeral. She'd stand beside my grave, tears rolling down her elfin cheeks, while she chucked spadeloads of earth on to the coffin lid and declared her undying love.

Only problem was: she loved someone else.

'What are you doing down there?' It was Pete.

'Thinking. Dreaming. Dying.' I stood up and told him about my brush with Death.

'That's a bit of a mess,' said Pete, and he actually looked quite knocked back. 'Darcy fancies Natasha, then?'

'Yep.'

'What does she think of him?'

'What do you think?'

'She's not going out with him, then?'

'No, but he's not going to just give up and go away, is he? You know what Darcy's like. And another thing, did you know Sky's got a boyfriend?'

'Really? Who?'

I shrugged. 'Haven't got a clue.'

'Bummer.' Pete stared into space for a bit. He wasn't his usual chirpy self at all.

'Let's face it, Pete, there's nothing here for us any more. I reckon it's time to hit the road.'

'Yeah, you're right.'

I told him about The Grange and the stockpile I was building up. He thought it sounded great.

'We could have everything ready by the end of the week.'

'Yeah.'

'We could make our break then.'

'Yeah.'

'What about Friday morning? First thing Friday morning. It'd have to be early, before anyone else is up and about. We don't want people asking questions. I reckon we should meet up about, say, five a.m., at The Grange.'

Pete nodded slowly. 'Five a.m., Friday.'

I smiled. This time it was for real, and I had Pete with me. Things would be so much better with Pete around. I'd have him to talk to, for a start, and I hate to admit it, but he was so much more grown up than me. He knew loads. He'd kissed a girl with tongues! (I don't mean she had more than one tongue—you know what I mean!)

'See what else you can get that could be useful,' I said as we parted.

'Yeah, OK. So Natasha doesn't like Darcy, then?'

'No.'

'What kind of person does she like?'

'I don't know and I don't care. Why?'

'Nothing,' said Pete. 'Just think she's a bit

77

weird.'

I drew a deep breath and let out all the air in my lungs slowly. Suddenly I felt very grown up and deep myself. I clapped a hand on Pete's shoulder. 'All women are weird,' I said.

## Pete's Tongue Experience

This happened one time when Pete was in America. His parents took him to a barbecue party. There were loads of people there and lots of kids. He took up with a girl called Prairie. They found a quiet place and sat down and talked for a bit and Prairie said she really liked his English accent and it made her shiver with delight. So he pretended he was James Bond. I said James Bond was played by Sean Connery and he was Scottish, but Pete said Prairie was American and couldn't tell the difference, so it didn't matter and I'd better shut up or he wouldn't tell me the rest of the story. Anyhow, Prairie got all overcome by his accent and they started kissing and she stuck her tongue in his mouth. I asked him what it was like.

'Liver,' he said. 'It felt like there was a big bit of liver in my mouth, only without the onions:

'That's revolting!'

'No, not really. It was quite nice liver.' Pete thought for a bit. 'I didn't chew,' he added apologetically.

**End of the Tongue Experience**

## 18

# EGG WHISKS VS BURGLARS

Natasha wanted to know how things had gone with Darcy, so I told her. I exaggerated a little (I said he'd killed me), because I wanted her to understand the full horror of what I had been through. She listened in stony silence.

'So, what am I supposed to do?' she asked crossly. So much for expecting sympathy.

'Don't ask me. Maybe you should tell your mum.'

'I don't think so.'

'Why not?'

'It will only make matters worse, stupid. Would you tell your dad?' One look at my face gave her the answer. 'No, I thought not. It's down to me, then.'

I couldn't think of anything to say. I mean, come on, what would you have done? I'd already been thumped once. I couldn't do any more. It was between Tasha and Darcy. I left her to it. I had a sophisticated escape plan to attend to.

I spent the next few days manically collecting equipment. This meant doing a lot of my snitching in the deep of night, when everyone was asleep. I kept my alarm under my pillow, set for 2 a.m. Then I'd get up and do my snitching runs. It made waking up in the morning hard. I was constantly tired.

The biggest problem was trying to avoid Pankhurst. That rabbit was a maniac. One night, just after 2 a.m., I was padding around the kitchen, and I opened the cupboard door and there was Pankhurst practically staring me in the face. How on earth did she get up there, for God's sake? She was four shelves up from the floor!

She hurled herself upon me and I staggered back with a giant white rabbit stuck to my head like some kind of exploding wig. I crashed into the sink, which was painful for me, but at least it had the effect of dislodging Pankhurst from my head. She fell straight into the sink and I quickly got the washing-up bowl, shoved it over her and she was trapped.

Everything went quiet. I wondered if rabbits were like budgies. Obviously they're not like budgies to look at, but budgies go to sleep if you put a cover over their cage. The washing-up bowl seemed to be having the same effect on Pankhurst. I crept back to bed as quickly as I could and had just reached safety when all hell broke loose downstairs. You wouldn't have thought a rabbit could make that much noise—not even a giant angora. Not even a radical feminist giant angora.

Dad was awake in a flash and he went charging down, closely followed by Tracey. They were not happy bunnies, and neither was Pankhurst. Ha ha.

At least my stockpile was growing quickly. I now had a frying pan, an assortment of knives, forks and kitchen utensils, the camping stove, a sleeping bag, two pillows and a pile of batteries I had carefully removed from various bits of equipment. (So the TV remote was dead.) Apart from the rabbit, I'd had no problems at all—until I ran into Natasha. That was a bit of a surprise.

It was about half past three at night and I was in

the process of removing the egg whisk from the kitchen as silently as I could manage. There was a scuffling noise from the hall, which I put down to the assassin rabbit, and I carried on. I had just managed to get the whisk out of the drawer without disturbing everything else, when I heard a sharp intake of breath. I froze and looked up.

It was Tasha. She stood there in her little shorts and T-top, staring at me open-mouthed.

'What are you doing?' we said in chorus.

'Getting a glass of water,' Tasha answered. Her eyes flicked down to the egg whisk. 'How about you?'

'Me too,' I said.

'With an egg whisk? Why are you holding an egg whisk?'

'I heard you coming.'

'What were you planning to do? Scramble me?'

'Obviously I didn't know it was you,' I said icily. 'I thought you were a burglar.'

'You were going to make the burglar into an omelette? Very brave. Totally stupid, but very brave. Trap his tongue in the beaters and whisk really hard. Brings tears to the eyes.' She stood at the sink, filling her glass.

'Have you spoken to Darcy?' I asked, trying to change the subject.

'I sent him a note. I said I'd think about it.'

'You're not really?'

'Of course I'm not. The guy's a creep. It's called playing for time.'

'So what will you do, eventually?'

'As if you care.'

'I'm . . . interested.'

Tasha went out to the hall and headed for the

81

stairs. 'I have a plan,' she murmured over her shoulder.

'Will it work?'

'Oh yes, it'll work all right.'

'Brilliant.'

Tasha was going up the stairs ahead of me. 'Yes—absolutely bloody brilliant,' she said, shutting her bedroom door behind her.

Then, in the morning I almost got rumbled by Sherry Trifle. She was hunting around the kitchen. 'I'll swear the small pan was here yesterday,' she said. Ha ha—wrong there, for a start, because I'd whipped it three days ago. La Trifle was obviously blind as well as stupid.

'Have any of you had it?'

'What for?' I asked.

'I don't know!' snapped Sherry. 'And where's the cheese grater? I've got a craving for cheese. I think it's the pregnancy. I need cheese. I need the grater.'

Just for once I didn't have a clue. Maybe Pankhurst had eaten it. But, come to think of it, I would need a cheese grater. I almost jumped up and said, 'Thank you! Good idea! I'll take it now!' Except, of course, it had been mislaid. Anyway, it would have been a bit of a giveaway. Plus the fact that I was never, ever going to thank Sherry Trifle for anything at all, except maybe for bringing misery, calamity and chaos into my life. Not to mention Natasha.

'Somebody must have seen the cheese grater. Tasha?'

'I'm not a cheese-grater person,' she said, which almost made me laugh. Almost. 'Perhaps you should look for the egg whisk,' she added, giving

82

me a little smirk.

Bat's buttocks! Surely Tasha didn't know? I'd seen her back to her bedroom. She can't have known I'd returned to the kitchen half an hour later and snaffled the whisk after all.

La Trifle huffed and puffed. 'Don't be stupid, Tasha. You can't grate cheese with an egg whisk. Do grow up.'

Tasha threw such a look at her mother and swept out of the kitchen.

La Trifle sighed. 'No pan, no grater. And the bread knife vanished yesterday.'

'Really?' I said, as casually as I could manage.

'Yes, really,' snapped La Trifle. 'This place is turning into a Bermuda Triangle for kitchenware. It's impossible to cook—there's nothing to cook with.' And she actually did that stampy thing. I'd always thought it was one of those things you only see on TV—you know, where the woman gets all cross and stamps her feet, waves her fists, shakes her hair, grits her teeth and goes 'Grrrrrrr!' But La Trifle actually did the full stampy-wavy-shaky-gritty-growly thing. Impressively silly it was too.

'I expect they'll turn up,' I said helpfully, and went upstairs. First thing I did was take the bread knife from beneath my pillow and put it in the rucksack. That was going to have to be moved tonight to The Grange, along with the whisk and the rolling pin—another item I reckoned would be useful.

I rang Pete and told him I'd nearly been discovered. 'How's it going at your end?' I asked. 'I've got so much stuff, Sherry Trifle reckons our kitchen's turned into the Bermuda Triangle.'

'Awesome! If she's right, you could have all sorts

of junk in there. Tell her to be very careful. You might discover Flight 19, that squadron of missing planes.'

'We have. They're in the cupboard under the sink.'

'Double awesome! Keep the door shut! Those pilots think it's 1943. The war's still on. If you open the cupboard they'll come whizzing out and bomb the lot of you.'

'I'll bear it in mind,' I laughed. 'Listen, where's all your gear? I haven't seen anything at The Grange yet.'

'It's all here,' he answered. 'Big pile.'

'What have you got?'

'Er, sleeping bag, clothes, shoes, um, tin of beans, bicycle pump—'

'What?'

Pete laughed. 'Joke. Haven't really got a bicycle pump. Haven't really got a bicycle. Did you see Natasha? What's she doing about Darcy?'

'She says she's got a plan that will work.'

'She's not going to go out with him?'

'No way.'

'Right.'

I told him how Tasha and I had met in the kitchen in the middle of the night.

'What—in her pyjamas?'

'Of course, Pete, it was night-time—not that she wears pyjamas.'

'No?'

'Shorts and T.'

There was a pause at the other end. 'That was a bit close,' he said at last. 'Her finding you like that.'

'I know. My heart was banging, I can tell you.

So, are you on for tomorrow morning?'

'Tomorrow?'

'It's Friday—the Great Escape.'

'Absolutely.'

'Meet me at The Grange about five o'clock.'

'Bit early. Are you sure you want to go tomorrow?'

'There's nothing here. We've got to go.'

'Right. Does she always wear shorts and T?'

'Who?'

'Tasha.'

'Not at school, no. What planet are you on? See you tomorrow'

'Right—and don't open that cupboard door.'


19

## RUNNING AWAY—THIRD ATTEMPT

It was done. We were going to go. It was impossible to sleep. I couldn't get comfortable, which was hardly surprising. I had the toaster stuck under my pillow. I'd decided to take it after all. I tossed and turned and kept looking at the clock. My head was full of stuff about my dad, my mum, my stepmother, my stepsister, Darcy, Delfine . . . Delfine! I hadn't said anything to her about going!

I sat up sharply. What would Delfine think? I slowly relaxed. It didn't matter. I wouldn't be around, not once Pete and I put our plan into action. Even so, it was a bit hard on her. Maybe I should leave her a letter? What was the point? She'd get used to it. She might miss me for a bit.

She'd probably be upset, maybe even cry a little after all, she really loved me. Would I miss her?

No.

I was going to miss Sky like crazy, which was stupid, since we weren't even going out together. And that was another good reason to leave. There was no way we could be together. She already had a boyfriend. I admired her loyalty, but it didn't do me any favours. There was nothing for me here any longer. I checked the alarm and drifted off to sleep.

I had a dream. It should have been about Sky. I would have liked to dream about Sky. But it was about Delfine, at least to start with. We were at school, in a cupboard, with the door shut. Don't even ask. How am I supposed to know why we were in a cupboard? It was a dream. I deny all responsibility. You can do that with dreams— thank God.

So, we were in this cupboard and I was drawing her. Yes. You guessed. And she started kissing me. And I was thinking (still in the dream, of course): this isn't liver and onions, this is pasta. Spaghetti. With curry sauce. And I was still painting her, only that was it—I was painting *her*. Painting her body. And suddenly it wasn't Delfine at all. It was Aunt Polly now, lying in the cupboard. (Obviously a very big cupboard.)

Anyhow, I crashed the Citroen and woke up, sweating. Weird. I bet Salvador Dali never had dreams like that. Maybe I was mutating into a surrealist. Maybe I'd wake up and discover I'd grown a weird moustache. I waited until I'd calmed down and then tried to sleep again. I'd hardly nodded off when the alarm went. Four

86

thirty. I was quite glad really.

I let myself out by the back door. Yikes, it was cold at 5 a.m.! But there was no turning back now. I crept along the street feeling incredibly guilty, as if my rucksack was full of stolen goods—which I suppose it was in a way. What would happen if I got stopped by the police and they searched me? How do you explain a rucksack full of egg whisks, rolling pins, casserole dishes and batteries? Luckily, the only person I saw was the milkman and he was too busy counting milk bottles and whistling out of tune. I hid behind somebody's front hedge until he'd passed.

The Grange looked more spooky than ever. I took a deep breath, made my way to the rear and went in. I checked behind the piano and was very relieved to see my stash lying there undisturbed. I sat on the floor, back to the wall, and waited for Pete. It was five. He'd be here soon. I looked at my pile and began to wonder how to get it all into my rucksack. I realized I might have to leave something behind.

Ten past five. I went to the dirty window. No sign of Pete yet. Maybe Aunt Polly was playing up. Pete once told me that sometimes she came in so late it was more like early in the morning. Another time she was so drunk she tried her key at the house next door. They'd shooed her away and called her a drunken old sot.

'Don't call me an old sod!' Aunt Polly had shouted back.

Half past five and still no sign of Pete. If he didn't arrive soon, we'd have to call the whole thing off. Either that or I'd have to go on my own. No, couldn't do that. I needed Pete to be there. He knew how to lure a seal out of its ice hole. I didn't think we'd ever find a seal, but Pete also knew six ways of making fire without matches *and* which cactus you could get water from if you were lost in a desert. He knew, because it had happened to him.

## Pete's Desert Experience

This happened when Pete was out in America visiting his parents last Christmas. They went off for a few days to look at the desert. They went to Death Valley, one of the hottest, most inhospitable places on earth. It was nothing but dry air, cacti, salt flats and rattlesnakes. The car broke down and they were stranded. Pete's dad said they had to stay with the car. That was what you did in a desert emergency. Don't wander off, stay with the vehicle. They boiled all day in the sun. At night the temperature dropped below freezing and they shivered.

The next morning they were still there. The sun rose higher and higher. They had long since run out of water. They thought they were going to die. An old man appeared, a local Native American. He said he was a shaman—a medicine man. He had a bent hat with an eagle feather sticking out of the band. His shoes were made from rattlesnake skins. He wore a buckskin loincloth. The old man kept pointing at his chest and saying,'Nykee. Nykee.'

'We thought it was his name,' said Pete. 'But he kept tugging at his shirt and grinning and suddenly my mum realized he was actually showing us the T-shirt. It was a Nike T-shirt. He was really proud of it.Weird!' Pete shook his head and went on. 'That man was amazing. He knew everything about the desert. He whistled at birds and knew what they said. He knew every animal, every plant. He could track an ant for days and hunt it down. But, most important, he knew where to find water. He took us to some cacti and sliced one open with his knife. It was brimming! And you know what the most incredible thing of all was? That old man was blind—blind as a bucket down a well.'

Much later a helicopter appeared and they were rescued. 'But if it hadn't been for that shaman,' Pete said, 'we'd have died.'

**End of Desert Story**

So, I really needed Pete to be with me. He knew important things. I decided to wait until six. If he didn't turn up by then I'd go back home and we'd try again another day. Something must have happened to him. Maybe Aunt Polly had caught him creeping out.

Six o'clock. No Pete. I decided to count up to 100 and, if he hadn't turned up, I'd go back home. I counted to 100. No Pete. I counted to 500, then unloaded my rucksack and crept home.

Everyone was still fast asleep, thank goodness, and no sign of Pankhurst. Bonus! I whizzed upstairs and undressed. I was just about to clamber into bed when the maniac rabbit launched herself at me from behind. Her paws raked into my shorts and the next thing I knew they were round my ankles and the rabbit was sitting in them. I could almost hear her laughing.

'If that's feminism, I don't think it's very civilized,' I muttered.

## 20

## MY BEST FRIEND?

So, I get to school and I'm half dead because I've been up since four o'clock in the morning, plus I've got paw scratches on my bum (again). They sting. Meantime, Pete's as fresh as a daisy.

'You look dead,' he said.

'Where were you?'

'Where was I when?'

'Five o'clock this morning. Remember?'

Pete frowned, scowled, rolled his eyes, looked at me and suddenly grinned. 'Oops. Sorry.'

'Is that all you can say?'

Pete shrugged. 'What do you want me to say?'

'Pete, I was up at four thirty. I waited at The Grange for two hours. It was our big day. We were supposed to escape.'

'I forgot. I overslept.'

'You're hopeless. Suppose Tenzing had overslept and stayed in his tent?'

'What?'

'Then Hillary would never have reached the top of Everest. Suppose Nelson had stayed in bed on the day of Trafalgar? He would never—'

'Have got shot and died!' Pete interrupted. 'See! Staying in bed can be a Good Thing.'

'I think you know what I mean,' I said icily.

'It was Aunt Polly's fault. She kept me awake half the night. So, sorry, I overslept. How's your sister today? What's she going to do about Darcy?'

'Don't ask me, and she's not my sister.

Stepsister.' I was pretty sure Tasha was in for a bad time with bully boy but I couldn't see that there was anything I could do about it.

'She doesn't like him, though, does she?'

'Not even Tasha could like Darcy,' I pointed out.

'Is she going with someone else?'

'I don't know! Who cares? Look, there's Sky—over by the science block.'

Pete grinned. 'She's awesome. You seen *Art Works?* That's her—Skysurfer. Cool.' I could feel Pete's eyes studying me.

'You reckon?'

'Course it is. And Obnoxx the Rather Unpleasant—brilliant!—that's Darcy.'

My heart started to beat faster. If Pete knew all this, what did the rest of the school know?

'Who do you reckon is doing it?' I asked, trying to keep my voice level.

Pete and I looked at each other. Time almost stopped. So did my heart. Pete raised his eyebrows.

'Could be anyone. I just hope they know what they're doing, because if Darcy finds out, he's going to be pretty mad.' Pete turned and stared out across the playground towards the science block. 'She is just so cute. Right! I'm going to go for it!'

My universe continued to crumble. My closest friend seemed to be bent upon ruining any chance I had of finding True Happiness. First of all, he couldn't be bothered to get up early enough to escape from the Gulag of Home Life, and now he was going to woo the girl of my dreams.

'She'll turn you down,' I said, without the remotest sense of conviction.

'Now, why would she do that?' Pete smiled. 'I'm

91

tall, dark, handsome, intelligent—'

'I refute it, thus! You're tall, dark and plug-ugly. She'll say no.'

'Maybe, but the thing is, you won't know unless you ask. Nothing ventured, nothing gained, as my wise old grandfather used to say.'

'Really? I didn't know you had a grandfather.'

'I have, but he's not wise, and he didn't say it. But had he been wise I'm sure he would have. It's the sort of thing wise grandfathers say. And now I must be off. I have a date with the most beautiful girl in school.'

Pete made a beeline for Sky. I watched miserably my heart thumping, bumping, lurching, having hiccups, sneezing, coughing and generally falling to bits inside my chest. Pete was talking to her. She tilted her head on one side, listening. She was smiling, nodding, picking up her bag. They disappeared round the corner of the science block. Together.

It was possibly the worst day of my life. The remainder of school passed in a kind of dreary fog. My brain had crashed. All it could do was replay that disastrous scene with Pete and Sky, over and over again. There was a moment in the replay when the film froze—the moment Sky smiled. I had never realized that a smile could pierce you like a dagger. When the smile was for someone else, it cut you into little shreds.

I suppose I should have been pleased when Delfine turned up and suggested we walk home together. She held my hand. I felt as if I was losing everything. I wanted to be walking home with Sky. I wanted to be holding Sky's hand. Delfine was my past, but now Pete had gone off with Sky and I had no future. Hell's telly! I was turning into a soap opera!

'You look fed up,' said Delfine, leaning her head against my shoulder as we walked.

'Bad day at the office,' I muttered.

'Want to talk about it?'

Tell Delfine! No way! My brain (the one that had crashed) tried to come up with something suitably disastrous and diverting.

'Had a test in French,' I lied. 'I got minus ten. Baguette was furious.'

'How can you get minus ten?' squeaked Delfine.

'By answering a question.'

'I don't get it.'

'It's simple. If I hadn't answered any questions I'd have scored zero, yeah?'

'OK.'

'But I *did* answer some questions. My answers were so bad I lost marks and ended up with minus ten.' Blimey. I'd almost convinced myself I really *had* taken a French test.

Delfine was frowning. 'I still don't—'

'Doesn't matter. It's just been a bad day.' Suddenly I was really tired. I didn't want Delfine hanging on my arm any more. I wanted to be at home, on my own. I shook myself free. 'I've got to go. I need some sleep.'

'See you tomorrow?' she asked, all wistful and doe-eyed.

'Sure.'

I hurried on without her, but after a few steps I took a glance back. She was walking away. I wished it was the last time. I wished I'd told her it was over. But she'd looked so desperate, as if I could crush her with a few words. I would have to tell her

93

sometime. And then, of course, there'd be tears and tantrums and . . . Darcy.

For now, though, it was time to hide away.

21

## TIME TO COME CLEAN

Wonder of wonders—the house was empty. No sign of Natasha. No sign of Sherry Trifle or Dad. No sign of Pankhurst. Maybe she was out in the garden, hunting rhinos. I had the place to myself. I walked into every single room making V-signs and blowing raspberries. Childish? I didn't care. I felt a whole lot better. Didn't do it in my own room, of course. Then I decided to be totally decadent and have a bath—a long, hot bath. I stripped off and was about to go through to the bathroom when I caught sight of myself in the long mirror on the back of my door. I stood there, looking at myself.

*This is me,* I thought. *I'm a stick insect.* I lifted my arms and flexed my muscles. Ha ha. What muscles? The hair in my armpits had grown even more. The sex-ed video we'd seen at school said that when girls grow hair during puberty they grow twenty metres of the stuff. Baboon's buttocks—twenty metres! Hope it doesn't all grow at once. I don't think it's an overnight job. I mean, you'd think people would notice, wouldn't you? The video couldn't even say how quickly boys' hair grew—it was obviously something too horrible to contemplate. It must be at least twice as much—forty metres. Forty metres! You could thatch a roof with that!

I had nothing like a roof on me—not even a small porch, not even enough to make a toupee for Dad's bald patch. My chest was puny and, generally speaking, I felt about as sexy as a combful of dandruff. I thought of Pete. He was much better built than I was. He was taller, stronger, better looking and he looked older. No wonder Sky went off with him. Groan groan. It was time to drown my sorrows in the bath, and quite possibly myself.

I locked the door, turned on the taps and waited for the tub to fill. My eyes wandered around the room. It was amazing how much stuff those women had brought with them. When it was just Dad and me we had soap and shampoo. Full stop. Soap and shampoo. Now there was so much bath foam and bath mix and moisturizer and shower gel and hair goo and heaven alone knows what. I was sure it was manufacturing itself. Or maybe all the bottles were secretly mating at night and producing baby bottles that grew during the day until they were big, adult bottles, and then *they* mated and produced even more bottles and the bathroom was slowly being invaded by a monstrous regiment of bottled bubbles in 100 different colours and smells. Awesome!

I sat on the edge of the tub, got a bottle of bath foam and tipped the contents alongside the running tap. Then I got another bottle and tipped that in. The water was already foaming up. I added a couple more bottles and, all of a sudden, the foam was everywhere, piling up and sliding over the top of the bath, down the sides and across the floor. Great bubbling peaks formed vast mountain ranges across the top of the bath and somewhere, beneath it all, was the bath water.

I hacked my way through the froth, plunging into it all and diving down into the warm water. My eyes began to sting. I rose up from under the waves and stood there, with foam piled up as high as my navel. I yodelled loudly. Then louder. I yelled out: 'I am the King of Froth and all must obey me or I shall fruth froth down your froat until you are fruffocated! Odle-layee-dee!'

'Simon? Is that you?'

Flying bumbits! It was La Trifle!

'Yes?'

'What are you doing in there?'

Now, excuse me a moment, but what on earth did she think I was doing in the bathroom? Ice-skating? Uncovering a long-forgotten Roman mosaic floor, cunningly concealed beneath the lino?

'I'm building a particle accelerator,' I said, standing there with froth up to my nipples.

'There's foam on the hall carpet out here,' said La Trifle.

Oh piddle. I tried to explain. 'That's what my particle accelerator does,' I said solemnly. 'It accelerates foam particles.'

'Have you been using my bath foam?'

'Only a tiny bit.'

'How come it's leaking out beneath the door?'

'It's leaking out?' I cried. 'Oh no! My particle accelerator has created Rogue Foam! Don't let it escape downstairs or the whole world will perish! For pity's sake, stop the foam BEFORE WE ALL DIE!'

It was a serious mistake to do this. I thought it

would amuse the Trifle. I thought I could make her laugh, jolly her along a bit, and then she'd go away. But, of course, you need someone with a sense of humour for that to work. No wonder it didn't. It only made matters worse. She hammered on the door so hard the towel fell off the hook.

'Let me in at once! I want to see what you're up to!'

'But I'm in the bath, nudely naked and nuddified.'

'Let me in!' (Hammer, hammer, hammer.)

I pulled the plug. I could hear water swirling out but the foam didn't budge. It just stayed there, a great mountain of the stuff. I tried to push it down the plughole. Have you ever tried pushing foam down a plughole? No? Well don't, because you can't. It's impossible. Your hands go straight through it. It really was Rogue Foam. I switched on the shower and tried to spray it to bits.

'Is that the shower you've got on now? What *are* you doing?!' screeched La Trifle.

'Having a shower,' I explained simply.

'But you've just had a bath.'

'I'm very dirty,' I said.

'Get out of there right now!' (Hammer, bang, hammer, bang.)

'I am getting out.'

I rushed to the window, flung it open, dashed back to the bath and began to scoop up armfuls of froth, carrying them across to the window and pushing them out. Some floated away on the breeze. Some clung to the house wall. Some fell into the back garden. I leaned out of the window and tried to give the bubbles a helping waft of wind by waving my arms around. A big wodge stuck on

97

the wall above the window. I stood on the bathroom stool and flicked at them, trying to get rid of all the evidence.

'Eeeeek! A flasher!'

How was I to know there was an old lady pruning in the garden that backs on to ours? Not my fault—she shouldn't have looked. Anyhow, I was busy wafting foam.

I yelled back at her, 'I refute it, thus!' And slammed the window shut. Oh God, how was I ever going to escape from all this?

'Open this door!' (Bang, bang, bang, bang, bang.) I grabbed a towel, slid back the lock and La Trifle practically fell into the room.

'*&?%$£@! %?& £$% *&& @?%!!'

Why is it that when I use words like that there's Big Trouble? Now I *hadn't* used words like that and I was *still* in Big Trouble. To make matters worse, Tasha arrived back, heard all the shouting, came upstairs to see what was going on and joined in—on her mother's side.

'Where's my tomato-and-ginger moisturizer? Have you used ALL my prune-juice-and-lizard's-lymph body scrub? Are you some kind of weirdo?'

What? Spawn of Trifle was calling *me* a weirdo?

'You're going to pay for all this,' La Trifle seethed.

Oh, but of course. I, with my millions of dosheroonies in the bank, my twenty offshore holdings, not to mention my secret account in Switzerland, would pay for everything. Just like that. I don't think.

I am pleased to say that I didn't lose my cool. I held my head high and walked proudly from the bathroom.

Tasha called after me. 'And by the way,' she sniped, 'if you're going to wrap yourself in a towel you want to make sure it goes right round your body. We can see your bum.'

Huh! How my life goes. I locked myself in my room, got out my sketch pad and set about the next stunning episode of Skysurfer.

22

## HAPPY HOME

Dad was not happy. Tracey wasn't happy. Tasha wasn't happy. I was . . . unhappy. So there we were in our Happy Home, staring and glaring at each other.

'Can't you, at least, try?' pleaded Dad.

'Try what?'

'I know this is an awkward time for all of us, but it wouldn't be so bad if we all tried to be useful.'

'Getting my stepmother pregnant is useful?'

'How dare you speak to me like that!' snapped La Trifle.

Dad's forehead went all wrinkly. I could see he was concerned. I felt half angry with him and half worried for him. No, actually it was about two-thirds anger and one-third worry. Well, maybe three-quarters anger . . .

'Tracey and I love each other,' said Dad simply. 'You two can't change the way we feel. Tracey is having our baby—*our* baby and since you are part of me and Natasha is part of Tracey, the new baby will be part of all of us.'

99

'That's interesting logic,' Tasha observed tartly.

'And that's enough from you,' La Trifle shot back.

I escaped upstairs. I'd been surprised by the exchanges between Tasha and her mum, but there were other things on my mind. I shut my door, put on some music, threw myself on my bed and had a think.

I thunk like crazy. I thinked and thunked and thonked for ages. There were things about Pete that were niggling me. First there was that business with Aunt Polly and not being able to shack up at his place. Then there was his slightly disappointing (to say the least) failure to turn up at The Grange. Finally, he'd gone off with Sky. And that was annoying. A lot.

So my state of affairs came to this:

1. Pete was up my nose and still climbing.
2. There was nothing at home for me.
3. There was nothing at school for me.
4. There was no life without Sky.
5. So, basically, my future here was nothing.

Conclusion: I was going to have to leave home on my own. Cue downbeat heavy music:
**Dum dum dum DUUUMMMMM!**

This was serious. All the time I had been planning to escape with Pete I hadn't really bothered to think in much detail. I'd assumed that Pete would come up with all the answers. After all, he always seemed to know what to do, even if it meant going off with the one girl his best mate fancied. Damn Pete. Damn damn damn him to bits. He would have been company, someone to share problems with. Now I was on my own.

Most of my stuff was already at The Grange. Once I'd got a few clothes together and some personal things, that was it. Ready to roll. So, where to after I had collected my kit from the old house? Leave town. Hit the road. Maybe I could get a coach out. Once I felt far enough away I'd get a job. Find a room somewhere. Start a new life. Yeah! Somewhere I could be myself at last. I was fed up with adults who only thought about themselves.

I knew it wouldn't be easy. There'd be a lot of walking with a heavy load. I'd be sleeping rough. I'd have to toughen up. That stick insect I'd seen in the bedroom mirror wouldn't make it. Exercise—that was what I needed.

I got down on the floor. Fifty press-ups: that'd toughen me up for a start. Phew. I was knackered after seven. What about that load on my back? I couldn't practise with my rucksack because that was already at The Grange. I scoured the room and eventually found my old sports bag under the bed. I tried filling it with clothes, but it wasn't heavy enough. I shoved my hi-fi speakers in the bag. That was much better. One, two, three—Oof! Hoisted the bag on to my back. It weighed a ton. OK, walking. I held the straps tightly and set off across the room. Halfway, there was a great yank on my back and an enormous crash. I staggered round.

My hi-fi was lying in pieces on the bedroom floor. Might have been a good idea if I'd unplugged the speakers first.

The door burst open and Dad hurtled in. 'What

101

was that noise? You all right? Good God, what on earth are you doing?'

I stood there with my bulging sports bag on my back, trailing two long leads, still connected to the disembowelled hi-fi, now spread halfway across the bedroom floor.

Dad straightened up and took a deep breath. 'For a split second I was worried. But no, why waste my breath? Aren't you a bit old to be having temper tantrums?'

'I wasn't,' I answered, sounding exactly as if I was.

Dad spread his arms wide. 'What's all this, then? Why smash your CD player?' He frowned. 'And why do you look like the Hunchback of Notre-Dame? What's that on your back?'

'I was lifting weights.' Hmmm, not bad. It was even fairly close to the truth. I was quite pleased with that one.

Dad blinked at me. He opened his mouth to say something, shut it, shrugged and went away. I put the hi-fi back together. Didn't work, of course.

That night I tried sleeping on top of the wardrobe. Obviously, I was unlikely to find a wardrobe in the middle of nowhere, but it was the closest I could get to the sort of situation I might have to deal with. Have you ever tried sleeping on top of a wardrobe? Don't, that's all I can say. Mine wasn't even a double. There was a piddling amount of room.

Tasha came in without knocking, as per usual. 'I heard strange noises,' she said. 'What are you doing up there?'

'Trying to sleep,' I said, because I knew she wouldn't believe me.

'You're scared of Pankhurst!' she chortled.

After she'd gone I got down and tried to sleep inside instead, but it was cramped and every time I moved the empty hangers jangled. It was like having your head stuck in a giant wind chime. I wondered if maybe there was some way I could attach myself to one of the hangers and then just dangle from the clothes rail, fast asleep, like a bat, only the right way up.

Eventually I got out and slept on the floor and pretty hard that was too. I must have fallen asleep because Dad had to wake me in the morning.

'What happened to you?'

'Fell out of bed.'

'Why didn't you get back in?'

'Must have knocked myself out when I fell.'

'How come all your bedding fell with you, your pillows landed under your head and your covers landed neatly on top of you?'

'I was unconscious. I don't know Maybe I was sleep-falling.'

'Sleep-falling?'

'Like sleep-walking, only falling instead.'

'Si, do you think you might be going mad?'

'I was confused, Dad, OK? I'm fourteen. I've got rampant testosterone doing strange things to my body, forty metres of hair sprouting from every hole and embarrassing growths at unexpected moments. Right?'

That scared him off.

## 23

# RUNNING AWAY—FOURTH ATTEMPT

Ha ha ha! I've got this book, a survival handbook.
It's about what to do in all sorts of emergency
situations. So, one of the things it tells you is how
to jump from a motorbike into a car. It's brilliant.
It gives you really useful instructions like: *Get the
bike as close to the car as you can.*

I'd never have thought of that in a million years.
I'd probably have the motorbike on an entirely
different road, going in the opposite direction, on
another day.

Here's another one: *Make sure the car window is
open.*

Really? Like I was going to hurl myself into the
car through a closed window!

And how about this staggering piece of info:
*This manoeuvre is best attempted at low speed.*

Flying bumbits! Who'd have thought it? And if
you want to be really safe, try doing it when
neither vehicle is moving. Or get someone else to
do it. And, anyhow, what do you do if you've got a
gigantic rucksack strapped to your back?

I guess it's quite a useful book really. I was
reading it to get ready for the Great Escape. It
tells you how to make snow caves to shelter in and
stuff like that, so it could prove a lifesaver. Think
I'll stay clear of bike-to-car transfers, though. (And
vice versa.)

Unfortunately it doesn't tell you what to do
when the old lady from round the back knocks on

the door and tells your dad that his son's been waving his thingy at her from the bathroom window.

'Simon!' I could tell by his voice I was in trouble. I headed downstairs, slowly.

Are you sure it was him?' asked Dad.

The old lady was astonished. 'I don't want an identity parade,' she twittered. 'It was him. He was standing at the window, stark naked, shouting and jiggling his . . . bits. And when I spoke to him, he said he was "futing it", the dirty beast.'

'Futing it?' queried Dad, eyes wide.

'Exactly. The beast.'

Dad turned, but didn't look at me. He seemed to be studying the carpet. Strange.

'Anything to say?' he croaked.

'I was having a bath.'

'You were standing at the window!' the old lady yelled.

'It was when I had that foam bath, Dad,' I explained, and I told him about shoving the froth out of the window

Dad kept putting a hand to his face and pulling at his nose—something I'd not seen him do before. 'So, it was accidental?'

'It was a froth emergency'

'Now I've heard everything,' the neighbour hissed. 'A froth emergency? Huh! You should be whipped.'

Dad saw her down the garden path, still arguing. When he got back he gave me a bit of an earful. As if it was my fault! He said I shouldn't have scared her. I said I didn't know she was going to be there and, anyhow, if that was all it took to scare her it was a wonder she'd lived so long. So Dad said I should show respect and I'm sure you can guess where the argument went after that. Finally, he asked me why there weren't any batteries in the TV remote.

'Maybe Pankhurst ate them,' I suggested.

Dad looked at the rabbit. It was, after all, a strong possibility.

I was glad to get back to my main task and over the weekend I made final preparations. I kept wanting to ring Pete to find out how things had gone with Sky but I *didn't* want to know as much as I *did*. If she'd agreed to go out with him, then it would only make my depression worse, and it was pretty unlikely that he'd been unsuccessful. Eventually I couldn't bear the suspense any longer—he was bound to tell me at school on Monday anyhow. I rang.

'Where've you been?' he asked. 'You must have sloped off pretty quick after school.'

'I was with Delfine.'

'Right.'

'How did things go with Sky?'

'Sky? Yeah, brilliant.'

'So, will you see her again?'

'Sure. I'll see her again on Monday. She's amazing. She let me—'

Click. I put down the phone. Couldn't listen to any more. A few seconds later it rang.

'What did you do that for?'

Click. I cut the call and switched off my mobile. Maybe Pete would get the message. I couldn't bring myself to tell him how I felt and what I thought of him. I was too churned up to speak. It could wait. Maybe I'd tell him on Monday. On the other hand, maybe I wouldn't be at school on

Monday. I could be on the road by the time school began. I could be on my way to a new life. Nothing to lose.

That night I did my final bit of foraging for supplies. It was 2 a.m., and this time I was mostly after food. I snaffled some tins from the kitchen cupboard and removed half the sliced bread from the bag. I got a little container full of milk, filled a water bottle, packed some eggs and bacon. I was about to head back to my room when I heard a door open upstairs and a shaft of light lit the top hall. I shrank back into the shadows, and one of the cans banged against the door. I froze in horror.

Upstairs, the light vanished and the door shut. Phew. Someone going to the loo. What was it with old people's bladders? I took deep breaths, waiting for my heart to subside before attempting the stairs. I crept up like a mouse, slipped into my room and silently shut the door. It wasn't long before I was asleep.

\*       \*       \*

Sunday breakfast was a strange business. Sherry Trifle wandered around the kitchen in an increasingly bad mood as she found more and more things missing.

'I'm sure we had bread. It's this bloody Bermuda kitchen again. It's driving me mad. Tasha, nip to the corner shop and get some more.'

'Why me?'

'Why not you? You're the only one properly dressed and we need more eggs. How come? I haven't used any for days. I thought I had half a dozen at least.'

107

Tasha got to the front door three times, only to be called back so that another missing item could be added to her list.

The rest of the day passed in a bit of a haze. There was one strange thing, though. I was lying on my bed, drawing a new Skysurfer episode, even though I didn't know how Miss Kovak would get it, unless I posted it to her. Anyhow, there I was and I felt this weight on the covers by my feet. I looked down and there was Pankhurst.

I stayed absolutely still, and for a moment or two so did the rabbit. We stared at each other. I waited for her to take a leap at my throat. I was thinking, when she leaps I have to wait until the last moment and then plunge my fist down her throat so she can't bite properly. (That wasn't in my survival handbook either, but I must have read it somewhere. Maybe it was one of those Famous Five adventures I read when I was small.)

Pankhurst moved. Slowly. She spread her giant body over my feet, settled herself and closed her eyes.

I was astonished. I could have sworn she was purring, except rabbits don't purr. I could feel the enormous warmth her body gave out as she sat on my feet, as if she were trying to hatch them. I couldn't guess what she was thinking but it was almost as if she was saying: *OK, let's call a truce. I know you're pushing off early in the morning, so just this once I'm going to be nice to you.* She stayed there an hour and a half.

I was all geared up now for my big break. I went to bed early. I set the alarm for four and tried to sleep. Why is it that when you desperately want to get some rest, when it's so important to you, you can't do it? My mind went over and over all my plans, all the details, and then all my hopes. Huh. That took all of two minutes. Sleep.

God that alarm was loud! Beyond the window was a dry, brightening dawn. I dressed, grabbed the bag of food and crept from the house. The birds were singing. The sun was rising. A fresh new day and a fresh new start. This was it! The Great Escape. (Again.)

The Grange looked as spooky as it always did. I was beginning to grow quite fond of its eerie atmosphere. At least that was how I felt until I got inside. I was hauling my rucksack out from behind the broken piano when I heard a strange scraping noise from somewhere deep inside the house. Something was moving about. Probably an animal, I thought: a fox or a cat.

Then it grunted. Cats don't grunt. Foxes might grunt, but it didn't sound like a fox grunt. There was more scraping. There was definitely some sort of living creature moving about in another room. Ghosts? Ghoulies? The triplets coming back to haunt their old home?

I tiptoed to the door. There was more grunting and scraping and by this time I was pretty certain there was another person in the house. A tramp? I made my way carefully down the hall towards the noise, watching where I put my feet. So far my survival handbook had proved to be totally useless. There hadn't been a thing on *What to do if you hear a strange noise in a weird deserted house.* I thought, *If I ever get out of this alive, I shall write my own book, all about how to run away and survive.*

'God!'

A voice—angry, fed-up, frustrated. I crept

closer. Someone was in one of the big rooms ahead of me. A faint shadow flickered through an open doorway. I edged towards it.

'Nnnng!' The word was almost spat out.

I reached the door, peered round and that was when I cried out, 'Tasha!?'

# 24

# MORE REVELATIONS

There was an enormous crash as Tasha dropped the rucksack she'd only just succeeded in lifting from the floor.

'Si?!'

'What the hell are you doing here?'

Tasha paused a fraction as if she'd been caught in the act—which she had—and then her face switched from confusion to anger. 'No, you tell me first. What are *you* doing here?'

I don't know why I'd bothered to ask, really. It was perfectly clear what she was doing. I suppose I was just surprised. Well, you would be, wouldn't you? There you are, with this great plan—*I know, run away from home and my horrible new stepfamily*—and then you find your horrible stepfamily running away from home to avoid . . . you? Did I mean *me?* Is that what Tasha was doing? Running away from me? Killer!

Tasha eyed me furiously. 'I might have known it'd be you. You ruin everything in my life.'

'Me? What about you?'

'What about me?' Tasha demanded.

'This was my idea. You're not supposed to be here.'

'Oh, excuse me. Think you're the only one allowed to run away? That's typical male thinking, that is. Totally thoughtless of other people.'

We stared at each other, all frowns and hunched shoulders, jutting jaws and clenched fists. My eyes fell on her rucksack. Elephant's pants! It was even bigger than mine.

'You'll never carry that,' I said.

'Oh really? You reckon?' She grabbed the straps and with an immense effort swung it on to her back. The sheer momentum of it all spun her round, right off her feet, and sent her crashing to the ground. She lay on her back like an overturned tortoise, feebly waving her arms and legs.

'Help me up,' she hissed, and I grabbed her by one hand. 'Just . . . help . . . me . . . up!'

That was when we started to giggle. We couldn't stop. Our laughter swept away the silent shadows of the old house. I had to leave Tasha lying there. I was laughing so much I didn't have the strength to help her.

She tried to speak. 'I . . . I bet I've broken all my eggs now!'

And we started laughing all over again.

'Your eggs!' I spluttered. 'I've been pinching them too. No wonder your mum ran out! I suppose you took bread as well?'

Tasha nodded and shouted, 'The egg whisk—I wanted that! God, the house must be empty. They'll think they've been burgled!'

'Strange burglars,' I said. We lapsed into a rather thoughtful silence. I had to ask her why she was running away.

111

'You were always arguing with me.'

'You were arguing with me,' I said defensively.

'And you've been drawing all those pictures about me and calling me Trash.'

'You knew that was me?'

'Everyone knows,' muttered Tasha. She sighed. 'OK, we were arguing with each other. And Mum kept telling me off because I was snapping at your dad, but he's not my dad, is he?'

'Same for me and your mum.' I nodded.

'And Darcy.'

'Darcy?'

'He wants me to go out with him. I don't like him but he won't leave me alone and I didn't know what to do any more.' Tasha paused to get her breath. 'And there was nobody I could talk to,' she said slowly.

'This is stupid.' I was thinking that all along we'd both been in the same boat and it was probably the *Titanic*.

'I know. What are we going to do?'

'Go back? Don't think I really wanted to run away anyway. I was dreading it. Pete was supposed to come with me.'

Tasha's head jerked up. 'Pete?'

'Yeah, but he was too chicken.'

'More like too muddled,' said Tasha. 'He can't tell fantasy from reality.'

'How do you mean?'

'All that stuff he makes up,' Tasha answered.

'What stuff?'

'Those stories he tells everyone about his aunt and her car and the things he's seen and done.'

Beaver's buttocks! It had never, ever, ever occurred to me that Pete was inventing it.

'He's just trying to make himself interesting,' Tasha suggested. 'We've all done it.'

'Have we?'

'Yeah—made things up to make ourselves look bigger, better—whatever. It's like wearing a push-up bra with added padding.'

'It is? Like a push-up bra?'

'Same principle. The bra's just a metaphor.'

I went quiet. I was thinking of that metaphorical bra, but it rapidly stopped being metaphorical and became a real bra instead and there was a real person inside it. She was very nice too, quite possibly Sky. My androgens were at it again. And the Citroën.

'What do we do now?' Tasha asked.

Pop! She'd gone. Shame. I glanced at my watch. Half five. 'Go home? Nothing has happened. We go to school and we stick together. If Darcy tries to make trouble, there'll at least be two of us. And we stick together at home too.' I scuffed the floor with one foot. 'I didn't realize home was horrible for you as well.'

'I hated you. You did such stupid things, you even used up all my bath stuff. You made me want to laugh and I hated myself for wanting to laugh at you and I hated you even more for making me hate myself and—well—bit of a mess.'

'Yeah. Come on. Let's go home.' We went to the door. 'After you, sis.'

Tasha managed a little smile.

## 25

## TOILET TROUBLE

People are like icebergs. I don't suppose you know that. It has only just occurred to me. I'll tell you what I mean. When you see an iceberg floating along (as you do, if you happen to be an Inuit), what you actually see is only one-tenth of the iceberg. Only one-tenth of an iceberg sits above the waterline. The other nine-tenths remain hidden below. It's no wonder the *Titanic* got ripped apart.

And that makes me think of other floating objects, like ducks. Maybe, when you look at a duck, you can only see one-tenth of it. Maybe nine-tenths of the duck's body is hidden beneath the water. Think of that—gigantically obese ducks with massive waddly bums and huge paddling feet. Next time you see a duck, take care.

Anyhow, I was saying that people are like icebergs. We only see a little bit of them. There's so much more to people than what we see. And I was beginning to discover this with Tasha.

Strange how quickly things can change. By the time we reached home Tasha and I seemed to have gone from worst enemies to best friends. I found this oddly encouraging. It felt like I was Popeye and I'd just swallowed six cans of spinach. I could tackle anything now, even Darcy. If he tried anything I'd simply smash him to a pulp. Just like that. It wouldn't be me lying on the ground, writhing about. It'd be him. And I'd say, 'You try anything on me or Tasha again and you'll need your coffin, Darcy. Understood?' And he'd barely be able to nod before he crawled away in a trail of blood and guts. Oh yes. No probs.

Later on, I came to a decision. Actually, I came to more than one decision—one of them being not to make too many decisions—but of the ones I had decided to make, the most important was that I was going to dump Delfine. Obviously, I wasn't going to walk up to her and say, 'Hey, babe, you're dumped. You and me are history. Our relationship has been tossed into the Black Hole of Dead Romance.' I'm not that cruel. Even so, there was no pleasant way. I wasn't looking forward to it.

So, when Tasha and I were walking down the corridor and found ourselves marching straight towards Delfine and Darcy, I made another quick decision. This was definitely not the moment to break up with Delfy. This was the moment to scarper double quick. Was it the red-eyed hurt splattered across Delfine's face, or was it the invisible multibarrelled, semi-automatic, hydrogen plasma, total-devastation gun that Darcy would have been carrying if there was such a thing? As it happened, his two fists were doing a pretty good impression of what was going to happen to me if I got too close to him. He was banging them together like giant rocks, cracking his knuckles. And he looked ginormous! He'd been so much smaller when I'd beaten him up in my head. The real Darcy was awfully big and awfully real. As soon as he saw us he shouted.

'Dingoid! Come here!'

I grabbed Tasha by the arm, whirling round and pulling her after me. Darcy yelled something with lots of asterisks in it and came charging after us.

There was no way we could outrun him, but I was hoping to find an escape route. It was just my luck there was nothing except the boys' toilets.

'It's our only chance!' I panted, shoving open the door and making sure the room was clear.

The door banged shut and suddenly all was silent apart from the hissing of the flush pipes and the slow trickle of water into cisterns. The windows were high, narrow oblongs, so no chance of climbing out. We were as good as trapped. I yanked open a cubicle door and pulled down the lid.

'Stand on that,' I whispered, 'and don't make a sound.'

We stood there, huddled together, arms clasped tightly round each other, too scared to feel awkward. The outer door burst open and Tasha's fingers dug into my back. I bit my lip to stop any noise coming out.

'They must have gone somewhere!' roared Darcy. 'Oi! Who's in there?'

The cubicle door banged and rattled.

I took a deep breath and dropped my voice as low as I could. 'Naff off, Darcy, you dingoid, or I'll make your brains into kebabs.'

'Who's that?'

'Hammerhead.' (Hammerhead was Wayne Hammersley's nickname—the most feared boy at school.)

'Oh. Sorry, Hammer.'

'Naff off,' I growled.

Darcy grunted. The door banged but we stayed on the toilet seat, giving everything a bit of time to settle.

116

'Has he gone?' whispered Tasha.

'Yes.'

She gave a tiny giggle. 'We can't go on meeting like this.'

We stepped down just as the main door banged open again. We caught our breath. Our feet and legs were showing and it was too late to do anything about them.

'Now, there's a funny thing,' said a strong Scottish accent, which meant it could only be Mr Stewart, chief caretaker. 'Four feet in one cubicle. I've never seen a laddie with four feet before, let alone with trousers on one set of legs and socks on the other.'

A key turned in the lock. The door opened.

'My, I've seen some strange goings-on, but this is the first time I've seen a courting couple in a toilet. It's hardly romantic. Could you not find a better place? I don't know what you kids will think up next. You'd better get yourselves to the head's office and explain yourselves.'

So we escaped Darcy only to end up in front of the head teacher, Mr Prendergast. He was not impressed. 'I get so very tired of dealing with this kind of activity. Don't you ever think of anything but snogging and sex?'

'But she's myow—' I winced as Natasha kicked the back of my leg. It really hurt.

'Sorry, sir,' she mumbled.

'It's all very well to say "Sorry", but where are your morals, girl? You can't behave like this or the next thing you know you'll be pregnant. Then what?'

'I don't know, sir,' Tasha muttered.

'Neither do I. Neither do I. We all like a kiss and

a cuddle but, please, really, standing in a toilet cubicle? Is that the best you could do?'

I wasn't sure if we were supposed to answer this or not, so I kept quiet. Besides, I was haunted by the image of the head having a kiss and a cuddle. Anyhow, Tasha seemed to be handling things, so I let her get on with it.

'We're very sorry, sir. It won't happen again, sir.'

The head suddenly looked tired. 'Oh, go away,' he sighed, waving a hand at us.

Outside his office I nursed the bruise on the back of my leg.

'Sorry,' smiled Tasha. 'I just thought that if he had known that we are almost brother and sister he would have gone ballistic. It was better to let him think . . . you know.'

'Good call,' I agreed. 'I don't suppose I'll be out of action for long.'

'Isn't that Darcy over there?'

'Where?' I cried.

'Don't panic. He's busy. Looks as if he's with—'

'Sky!' I gasped. Ever seen all your most wonderful dreams sucked into a Black Hole? It had just happened to me and it wasn't nice. I couldn't bear to look and I couldn't bear to take my eyes off them. They were chatting like they were best buddies. He touched her arm. My heart turned to ashes and I turned away.

Later that morning Pete tracked me down.

'Haven't seen you for ages,' he grinned. 'What's up?'

'Not a lot.'

'Got some good news,' said Pete.

'Really? What can it be? Sky's dating every boy in school? You've been to an orgy with six nuns?'

Pete pulled a stern face. 'I refute it, thus! What's got into you?'

'Doesn't matter.'

Pete studied my face for more information but soon gave up. 'Yeah, got some good news,' he repeated. 'Aunt Polly's agreed I can have a party at my place—her place.'

'Right.' And I was thinking: *lovely, just what I need; a nice jolly party where I can watch Sky smooching in the corner with—who? There were so marry to choose from these days. Her boyfriend? Pete? Darcy? How wonderful.*

'It's going to be next Saturday. Aunt Polly will be there to keep an eye on things, but she's pretty cool, so it should be great. I'm inviting everyone.'

'Everyone?'

'You know, the crew. You, Tasha, Sky, Delfine, all the others. It's going to be the most megatastic party ever. Nathan says he's got some booze and I'm going to get some too.'

'Right,' I muttered. If Delfine was going, she'd bring Darcy. It seemed that my brushes with Death were getting closer and more frequent. Maybe this time he'd catch up with me. Maybe I wanted to die, even.

About the only good thing that happened was when Miss Kovak saw me wandering about aimlessly and came over especially to tell me that the school couldn't get enough of Skysurfer.

'It is such a hit, Simon. I hope you're pleased.'

'Sort of.'

'Everyone is talking about it, wondering who does it and trying to guess at the identity of the characters. They've all got Sky, of course, but they're not at all sure about the others. Who's that

119

little tubby man that keeps kicking things for some reason?'

'You'll have to ask Mr Hanson,' I said.

'Really? He's such a fan. I've never seen him laugh so much. What about Obnoxx the Rather Unpleasant? Would that be Darcy by any chance?'

'Yes.'

Miss Kovak put a hand on my shoulder and gave me a steady look. 'You be careful. Is Punykid going to make it? Will he find the secret Elixir of Preposterone?'

'Wish I knew,' I said.

But deep inside I was pleased. People were waiting to find out what was going to happen. It was an odd feeling. Was I making this thing up, or was it making up me? Prawns in pants! A comic strip was taking over my life!

On the way home I got a text from Pete. He wanted to go shopping for the party. Great. Maybe I could buy a subsonic plasma-annihilator gun so I could surprise Darcy.

26

CHUGGA-CHUGGA!

You can never find a subsonic plasma-annihilator gun when you want one. Pete and I went up and down the High Street. We trailed round and round The Mall. Pete tried on umpteen pairs of trainers. Don't ask me why. He didn't have the money for any of them.

'Yeah, I know, but you still have to know what

they look like.'

'They look like trainers.'

Pete looked at me and shook his head sadly. 'You are a disappointment to the God of Shopping. Come on, this party has got to be the party of parties! Girls and booze!'

'Don't you think of anything else?'

'Do you?'

Good question, so I ignored it.

'Is Tasha coming?' he asked.

'Why?'

'I saw you talking to each other the other day. You were laughing and you haven't slagged her off for at least forty-eight hours. What's going on?'

I told him about The Grange and how we'd sorted out a few things. 'Tasha's OK,' I said.

'Yeah? Guess so. What about Sky? Everyone's talking about you two at school. They reckon something's going on.'

'Wrong. She's got a boyfriend.'

'Really? Who?'

'Mystery man—no idea.' I watched his face closely but he wasn't giving anything away.

'And Darcy reckons he's Obnoxx the Rather Unpleasant.'

'Clever Darcy. Fancy spotting that! Everyone knows it's him.'

'Does Sky pose for you?'

'No!'

'Shame. I never knew your brain was so weird. Those elephants are mad!'

'Have you blabbed to anyone?'

Pete shook his head. 'And get you killed instantly? No way. But you'd better watch out. I think Darcy suspects.'

I held up a hand. 'Don't say any more. My head's full of nasty images already.'

'Being in hospital's OK,' Pete offered, by way of comfort.

'Great. How would you know?

'When I was three,' he said, very seriously, 'I was in a multiple pushchair pile-up.'

I had to laugh. I couldn't help myself.

## Pete's Multiple Pushchair Pile-up

This was long before Pete's parents went off to America. They went to a big shopping mall where there was a special event at one of the kiddy shops. It was going to be opened by TV's latest heart-throbs, Miles Better and Jemima Suffix. Then there'd be a demonstration of different disposable nappies.

Pete and his parents were halfway round the mall when an announcement said that Miles and Jemima had arrived and were about to open the store, and afterwards they were going to demonstrate the disposable nappies.

Instant panic. Half the shoppers seemed to think that the TV stars were actually going to model the nappies! Can you believe that? Instant mad dash by hundreds of shoppers down to the kiddy store. Since most of them had kids and pushchairs, it was a recipe for disaster.

Pete's parents got caught up in the rush. People were charging down the escalators from the floor above, shouting and yelling. Fists were flying as more and more people tried to cram into a smaller and smaller space. One pushchair locked wheels with another and, in trying to tear them apart, others got jammed and before you knew it there were pushchairs at all angles, blocking the escalator and the pile-up continued backwards, reversing up the escalator until it spilled right back on to the top floor. The pile was three pushchairs high in places.

Everyone was screaming. Someone pressed the alarm button and the escalator juddered to a halt. Pete's pushchair had fallen sideways and he'd been tipped out. (He wasn't wearing a seat belt.)

'I was run over by a twin-buggy,' he said. 'yelled so much, Mum and Dad thought I must have broken something. I was whisked off to hospital and had lots of X-rays and so on. But I'd just been very scared.'

### End of Pete's Story

'So, you never got to see Miles and Jemima modelling nappies?'

'No. Sad, isn't it? In here. I want to look at some jeans.'

We marched into a department store and we were making our way through the women's section when we came across Sky.

'Hey! Just the people I need!' she beamed excitedly.

'Really? Us?' Pete was grinning from ear to ear. He would.

'I'm trying to find something for the party,' said Sky. 'What do you think of this?' She held a crop top across her chest, moulding it to her curves with her hands.

I couldn't bear it. 'We've got to go—' I began.

'No, we haven't. Try it on,' said Pete.

'Good idea. I'm going to try these jeans too. Wait there.'

'What are you doing?' I asked Pete. 'We can't hang about here.'

'Why not?'

I gazed around. We were surrounded by women's things. We were right next to hangers full of bras and pants. I didn't know where to look. I kept thinking the assistants must be watching us, but if I didn't look at the bras, I was looking at knickers and if I wasn't looking at knickers, I was looking at other stuff that seemed incredibly small and skimpy.

'Hey, look,' said Pete, fingering some tiny pants. 'Do they really wear these things?'

'Put them back,' I muttered. 'Just try and be normal, will you?'

'What do you think, boys?'

It was Sky. She was back. My heart leaped into my throat. She looked fabulous.

'Give us a twirl,' said Pete.

'Pete!' I hissed, but I watched, mesmerized, as Sky turned round.

She stopped and looked at Pete questioningly.

'Stunning,' he said, shaking his head in admiration. 'Totally stunning.'

'Stuff?'

'Hmm!' All I could do was grin and nod like some five-year-old's little plastic toy.

Sky pulled at the top. 'It's not too tight?'

'No.' I swallowed, coughed, choked and went red.

Sky giggled. 'Thought I might try a bikini,' she said.

124

Pete's eyes popped. God knows what mine were doing—cartwheels probably.

'But they haven't got any,' she added. 'Oh well, think I'll get the top. Thanks for your help. See you tomorrow.'

Off she went, leaving Pete and me saturated with every male hormone known to science, plus several more yet to be discovered. We could have sold our bodies for Science And The Good Of The World. We might have ended up having newly discovered hormones named after us, like Stufferomone and Peteromone, instead of which we just stared after Sky, in a happy trance.

'Are you going to buy those knickers?' an assistant demanded. 'Or are you just resting your hand there?'

Pete drew himself up and looked the assistant squarely in the eye. 'I refute them, thus!' he declared, whisking his hand away from the display.

Then we fled. Stiffly.


27

## HOLY SOCK!

'You can't go to a party on your own,' the Trifle told Tasha.

'I'll keep an eye on her,' I offered.

'I thought you two couldn't stand the sight of each other?' The Trifle remained suspicious.

'Si's OK.'

Tasha's mother shot me a look. Scorn with raised eyebrows.

'Women,' I joked. 'Always changing their minds.'

You might have thought that by now I would know it was always a Seriously Big Mistake to joke with a pregnant Trifle. The Trifle did not have a sense of humour. What the Trifle did have was a Seriously Withering Stare. She switched it on, powered up, looked at me and pulled the trigger: 'And what exactly would Mr Fourteen-Year-Old-Adolescent-Boy-Child know about women?'

'Dangerous,' I hazarded. 'And to be treated with respect.'

The Trifle continued aiming her Seriously Withering Stare at me, but I could see I'd managed to take the sting out of it. 'You'd better make sure you do,' she grunted.

'I'm cool,' I said.

'Cool is what you're definitely not,' muttered the Trifle. 'Anyone who can use up four entire bottles of bath foam in one go *and* outrage an old lady is definitely not cool.'

'It was only bubbles.'

'Expensive bubbles!'

'I said I was sorry. So, can we go to Pete's party?'

'You'll have to check with your father, but I suppose it's OK with me. There won't be alcohol, will there?'

'Fat chance,' said Tasha.

'Good.'

So, then Tasha had to spend ages deciding what to wear. She kept popping in and out of my room with a bewildering array of outfits, all of which looked fine to me. It was OK but it wasn't eye-popping, like Sky's display. That still made me feel hot all over.

'What do you think of this?'

'It's OK.'

'It's no good saying "It's OK" all the time.'

'Everything I've shown you has been "OK" so far.'

'But they are OK. What else do you want me to say?'

Tasha sat on my bed next to Pankhurst and crossed her legs. (Yes, you did read that right. The radical feminist rabbit was on my bed again. She was making quite a habit of it.) 'Listen, this is how it is. There'll be boys at this party, right, and girls. So promise you won't laugh . . .'

'I promise I won't laugh.'

'Swear you won't make stupid noises or pull stupid faces . . .'

'Tasha!'

'Swear!'

'OK, I swear on this sock . . .'

'What's so special about that sock?' demanded Natasha.

I pushed a finger through a hole in the toe. 'Bless you, my child, it's a holey sock,' I pointed out. 'It's the Holey Sock of Stuff.'

'Fine. Take the oath.'

'I swear on this holey sock that I won't whatever it was you asked me to swear.'

'OK.' Tasha bounced on the bed a bit and resettled herself 'It's like this. It's a party—'

'Get on with it!'

'And the boys will be after the girls, and the girls will be after the boys.'

'Maybe.'

'So, if you want to get someone in particular you have to put on a show. It's no good being "OK".

127

You have to look so giga-brilliant that the person you're after can only see you.'

'Right.' We looked at each other for several seconds. 'So, what you're saying is that you want to look good because there's someone you're after at the party?'

Tasha blushed.

I'd rumbled her. 'So, who is it?'

Silence.

'I won't tell anyone.'

'I know you won't because if you do I shall remove your head without your permission. Pete.'

'Pete! My friend Pete?'

'Why so surprised?'

'You can't trust him, Tash. He makes things up. You told me that yourself.'

'He's muddled, that's all.'

'He stole Sky from me.'

'How do you know that?'

'He asked her out and she went off with him.'

'Pete's going out with Sky?' Her face fell. 'I didn't know that. Are you sure? I thought . . . oh well, never mind. I'm not going to give up on Pete, and you shouldn't either.'

'But I don't want to go out with Pete.'

'Stupid! You know what I mean. Maybe you should try asking Sky again.'

'I've got to dump Delfine first.' I pulled a face. 'I don't want to hurt her.'

'Sorry,' Tasha said brightly. 'Unavoidable. She'll get over it.'

'I know, maybe, but . . .'

'Look, Si, you're doing the right thing in the long run. At least you're being honest with her. There's no point in carrying on with someone when you don't love them any more.'

I paused a second and then said, 'Does that include adults?'

Bang! It was like I had just hit both of us on the head with a brick. It was almost exactly what Dad had said to me when he and Mum split up. For a few seconds Dad and I and Tash and Tracey were all sharing the same world and it wasn't very comfortable. Tash and I stared at each other in silence. I wished we could un-think what we'd just thought, but now it was there.

Tasha let out a long sigh. 'You have to break up with Delfine and I've got to sort out Darcy, once and for all.'

'Why don't we do it at the party?' I suggested. 'That way we can do it together and Darcy won't be able to make a fuss because there'll be so many others there.'

'What about when we're back at school?'

I shrugged. 'All I know is that we can't spend the rest of our lives going about in fear of what Darcy might do. We've got to face up to him. That's all there is to it.'

'That's all,' echoed Tasha glumly.


28

## DESTINY MAKES A MOVE

This is true: there was a man who had hiccups for sixty-nine years. Sixty-nine years! That's most of his life, and he'd be hiccuping no matter what he was doing.

129

Eating and hiccuping.

Sleeping and hiccuping.

Riding a bicycle, hiccuping.

Brushing teeth, hiccuping.

Having hiccupy dreams. (About not having hiccups.)

How can you possibly drink while hiccuping? He must have been such a mess—clothes covered with hiccuped sludge. Did he ever get to *snog* anyone? Supposing he didn't—that would be so sad. Maybe he met a hiccuping woman, but that would make things even worse. Unless they had synchronized hiccups. Kiss-hic! Hic-kiss!

Thinking about that man helped me to keep things in perspective. OK, so maybe Darcy was going to pulverize me, but at least I wouldn't take sixty-nine years to die of hiccups. Sometimes it's useful to bear in mind what others have to suffer.

Like poor Delfine, hopelessly in love with me. And I was going to break her heart, because ever since Sky had arrived at school I'd felt that my destiny lay with her. Sky was my other half. That was how it seemed, even though I hardly knew her and we had spoken so little. I just knew there was something there. And, of course, she was quite simply huggatastic. Every time I saw her my body turned into an entire biochemistry experiment and all sorts of weird things happened.

So Saturday came. I got out all my clothes and spread them around my room. Tash asked if I was having a spring clean.

'Trying to decide what to wear tonight.'

'Cool. I'll help.'

'No way!'

'Listen, let me show you what Sky most probably

likes. Is that a good idea or not?'

'Maybe. I withhold judgement for the time being.'

She picked out a pair of white jeans I'd meant to bin months back.

'I never wear those. Nobody wears white jeans!'

'And how many girls come running after you?' That rather floored me.

'I thought not. So wear these jeans and this T and this top. Try them.'

'Nobody looks like that!'

'Exactly. You have to stand out, Si. Everyone will notice you. Your male friends will probably laugh because you're different, but I reckon Sky likes different. So she'll think, hey, he's cute, he's cool, and he doesn't care what his mates think. He makes up his own mind. I like that. I want to be with him. I want to be close. I want to hold him. I want to kiss him. I want to—'

'OK! You've made your point!'

'Si—you're looking awfully flushed.'

'Yeah, and if you don't get out of my room at once you're going to look awfully dead.'

'Charming. You try to help and all you get are death threats. I don't—'

'OUT!'

I slammed the door and took several deep breaths. I got into the white jeans. I pulled on the T and tried the jacket. I stood in front of the mirror. I pushed my hair back. I did some dance moves. I fell over. Better try not to do that last bit at the party. I studied my reflection. A stick insect in white jeans. It was certainly different. But would it work?

I took my mind off the evening by starting to

draw the final instalment of Skysurfer. It was time for Punykid to face up to Obnoxx. In the drawings I was so powerful—I could make anything happen. I knew who was going to win, and I guess you know too, but my real-life battle was quite another matter.

The human body has two million sweat glands. Count them if you don't believe me. It's an awful lot and every one of mine seemed to be on turbo-boost as Tasha and I went into Pete's house. I had four things on my mind. (Multitasking! Maybe I was getting in touch with my feminine side—hopefully, not too much.) Anyhow, four things on my mind:

1. What would everyone (especially Sky) think of how I looked?
2. How would Delfine react when I told her it was all over? (I'd packed some pocket tissues to help out.)
3. Just how painful was dealing with Darcy going to be?
4. Sky? (A billion unanswered questions there.)

You could hear the din from the music system halfway down his street. Pete's Aunt Polly was at the door with a tall glass in one hand and her other round the waist of some hulk.

'Hi, Stuff, who's the beauty with you?'

'My sister—Tasha.' I was getting used to this. It sounded good.

Aunt Polly squeezed the hulk's waist. 'This is Ryan.'

'Nice,' Tasha observed.

'Hands off,' beamed Aunt Polly. 'Go on

132

through. Pete's out the back somewhere, chatting up the girls. Nice jeans, Stuff.'

Did she really mean that or was she being sarcastic? I couldn't tell from her smile and a second later Tasha was pulling me through to the back.

The place was heaving with bodies—upright, downright, sideright—some dingoid was even standing on his head. (He crashed to the floor a second later.) There seemed to be a lot of smooching going on in dark corners. In fact, I wondered if there were any dark corners free.

And a second after that I saw Sky. Dancing with Pete.

Have you ever felt you've just been hit, only you haven't? Like an invisible blow has knocked the wind out of you? Pete saw me and waved back wildly, a huge grin on his face. Sky glanced across and smiled.

Someone tapped me on my shoulder. I turned round.

Delfine and Darcy.

Darcy and Delfine.

My destiny.


29

TOOTHBRUSHES AND OTHER WMDS

**Some Interesting Information About the Appendix and Toothbrushes**
Here's a true story about the appendix and the First World War (1914–18—which, of course,

133

you knew). The appendix is that funny little bit of intestine that doesn't appear to serve any purpose, except that it goes bad sometimes and makes you so ill you have to go to hospital and have it whipped out. (I suppose it can be done at home on the kitchen table with a potato peeler and bucket, but hospital is advised.)

People have had all sorts of strange ideas about why people get appendicitis. Some thought it came from eating too many peas. Complete rubbish. And during the First World War the British soldiers thought it came from swallowing loose toothbrush bristles. More rubbish, of course, but that's what they thought, and they got this idea that the enemy were deliberately manufacturing toothbrushes with loose bristles and then somehow getting them sent to British soldiers. What a wickedly sneaky plot! As a weapon of mass destruction the toothbrush must have been quite awesome.

**End of Info About Toothbrushes, etc.**

So, face to face with Darcy I found myself wondering if there were any loose-bristled toothbrushes close at hand. Because I needed one. Desperately.

'Where have you been?' Delfine pouted. 'I haven't seen you for days. You haven't been answering your mobile.'

'Battery went,' I lied. 'Couldn't get a new one. Anyhow, I've been busy. Listen, Delfine, we've got to talk.'

I glanced up at Darcy. He gave me a big grin and drew a finger across his throat. Oh great.

'Can we go somewhere without your big brother?'

'Why?'

'So we can be private.'

'Don't trouble yourself, pustule,' chuckled Darcy. 'You're wasting your time.'

'I need to talk to you,' I hissed at Delfine. Damn! I wanted this to be civilized. I wanted Delfine to understand that I was upset too, but she was making it so difficult. Delfine folded her arms across her chest and cocked her head on one side.

'I don't see much point in talking,' Delfine said, examining her nails. 'I don't see much point in you at all, Simon. In fact, you're dumped. So there. Ta-ta.'

And that was it! She turned on her heel and swept from the room like the queen herself, except I don't suppose the queen wears slingbacks and has a butterfly tattoo on her bottom. (She'd never shown me. I said: 'What's the point in having a tattoo there if you're not going to show anyone?' The thought was driving me crazy. Didn't make any difference. She wouldn't show me. No chance of seeing the butterfly now.)

I didn't know whether to laugh, cry or what. It didn't matter, because I didn't have time to consider my reactions. Delfine might have gone, but Darcy was still there.

'Seems like my sister has finished with you, my cretinous crudbasket.' He grinned. 'However, it pains me to tell you that I haven't. Do you know what I have been living with for the last three days? A wet mess. I don't like it when my sister gets upset because what upsets my sister upsets me and that makes me feel even worse, and who's to

135

blame for all this? A mucoid piece of pus. How very selfish of you.'

Ballistic bums! This was a bit rich. I could feel resentment charging up my chest, up my windpipe and into my mouth—and that's where it all spilled out.

'Selfish? Me, causing problems? Listen, Darcy, it's you who causes the problems. You go round threatening everyone and beating them up if they don't do what you want. That's what I call selfish and causing problems. You're the problem round here, not me.'

The music had stopped. The party had stopped. My life was about to stop. Everyone seemed to have retreated to the sides of the room, leaving me and Darcy squaring up to each other. ( Just bear in mind he's much taller than me, and older.) He threw back his head and gave a snarling laugh.

'Look at you!' He pushed me back. 'Stinknoid!' Push. 'Reckon I'm stupid, don't you? Do you think I don't know who does those drawings? Think I'm so stupid I can't even recognize myself? Think I'm obnoxious, do you? Obnoxx the Rather Unpleasant? You don't know what unpleasant means, but you're going to find out.' Push.

I went back a step. My heart was thundering as I stepped forward again.

The room was absolutely still and silent. I could feel fifty pairs of eyes on us as we circled each other. My head was screaming: DON'T BE SO BLOODY STUPID, SIMON! But it was too late. I was angry, really angry. Everything wrong in my life seemed to relate to Darcy.

'Do what you like, Darcy, because it won't change anything important. You can't mess with my brain, whatever you do. So, as far as I'm concerned, you can get lost. In fact—' and I pointed at him as sternly as I could manage—'I refute you, thus!'

And I poked him. With my finger. I did!

I saw Darcy draw back his fist. Suddenly a wonderful aroma enveloped me. Someone brushed past and stood between us. It was Sky.

'Touch him and you're dead,' she said.

Darcy's eyes flicked around the room. I could see he was unnerved. He laughed again. 'Oh right. You and whose army?'

'That goes for me too,' said Tasha, stepping up beside me.

Darcy was sweating. He was hesitating. He didn't know what to do. Sky stretched out and touched his arm, gently.

'You don't want to do this, Darcy. You know you don't. Remember what we talked about?'

Darcy stared at her. And the way she was speaking to him—that was odd. Brainflash! *Was Darcy her boyfriend?* The one she wouldn't two-time?

'Go and quieten down. Enjoy the party. We can talk tomorrow.' Sky patted his arm again.

Something inside him switched off. He gave a tiny nod, turned and vanished into another room. Someone turned the music on again and slowly people drifted back into dancing and yakkety-yakking.

My legs were jelly and my heart was galloping. Galloping jelly—not a good combination. Sky and Tasha and I just looked at each other. We let out our breath. We raised our eyebrows. We began to smile a little and finally we laughed, more from

137

relief than anything else.

'Thanks for the rescue,' I said, my brain somewhat confused.

'Had to,' said Tasha. 'Couldn't let you do it on your own, not when I knew you were doing it for both of us.'

I gave Sky a small grin. 'You were pretty cool, jumping out from nowhere like that.'

'Come on, Punykid,' she said, 'I'm Skysurfer, aren't I? I had to.' She seemed quite small, serious. She wasn't smiling any longer—not superhero material at all.

'What was all that "we'll talk tomorrow" stuff about? Are you all right? Do you want to sit down somewhere?'

Sky nodded. The rooms were full of people and noise. I caught sight of Darcy sitting in a dark corner, alone, gazing at nothing. He didn't see us. Eventually we found the back garden and sat on a low wall, in silence at first.

'I was a bit scared,' Sky admitted.

'Me too. More than a bit. You OK now?'

'Yes. No. Some bits are, some bits aren't.'

'You're not making sense,' I said. 'What's up?'

'It's . . . I . . .' She shook her head. 'Doesn't matter. It's too soon.'

'You and Darcy—you know each other?' I held my breath, waiting for the answer, and when it came I suddenly knew what the *Titanic* felt like when it sank.

'Of course we do.'

Down I went, gurgle, gurgle, gurgle, all hands lost to the cold, icy North Atlantic Ocean, along with the sausages and the marmalade and the 36,000 oranges, 9,000 spoons, 20,000 bottles of

138

beer and 7,000 lettuces, among other items. Down I went, right to the very bottom of the sea and I lay there in the deepest, darkest, coldest, loneliest place on the planet.

## 30

## STUFF I DIDN'T KNOW

'We take classes together,' said Sky.

Did I hear that right? The *Titanic* slowly began to rise back towards the surface. (Along with 36,000 etc., etc., etc.)

'But he's older he's a different year group.'

'Learning Support,' Sky explained.

'Learning Support? You don't need Learning Support!'

'Stuff, you haven't got a clue. You don't know everything, and hardly anything about me. Darcy and I both have problems. I'm dyslexic and he's, well, a bit more complicated than that, but we do a lot of work together. He's screwed up, and he knows he's screwed up.'

'Everyone hates him,' I pointed out.

'He knows that too, and he hates himself. Imagine what that's like. That's why he gets so angry.'

I took a deep breath. At least by this time the *Titanic* was completely afloat. I suddenly remembered the note Darcy had sent Tasha, the one with the odd spellings. It made sense now. And getting me to read Tasha's note back to him. So that was Darcy explained.

Sky still seemed a long way away. I desperately wanted to help her. She obviously had a problem and maybe there was something I could do. Perhaps I should change the subject.

'You were so cool back there, when you jumped in front of me.'

'You already said that.'

'I know, but it meant a lot to me.'

'Really?' She suddenly gave a little smile, right at me. Biochemical experiments again. Phew! I had to take a really deep breath.

'I was pretty pleased to see you there.'

'You were?' That smile again. I struggled to think of something to say, anything, but my head was in a whirl. I was enveloped in her smell, floating in Paradise. I could feel the warmth coming off her body, so close to mine. She was looking right through my eyes and into my heart. She leaned towards me. Could I? Dare I? I closed my eyes.

Our lips touched. Yes!

And suddenly she pulled away No!

I opened my eyes and there she was, right in front of me, looking very alarmed. She drew back with a little shake of her head.

'Sorry. I couldn't help it.'

I touched her face with my hand. When I spoke my voice was a tiny croak, like I was a frog. 'It's all right,' I whispered. 'Everything's all right.' And we kissed again, properly.

AND SHE DID LIP-NIBBLING —JUST LIKE THE BOOK! SNOG OF SNOGS!!

So there we are. How my life goes. That was so, so good. Eventually we went back into the party and did some dancing and stuff (without falling over), but the snogging was the best bit. I just feel so comfortable with Sky, like we've know each other all our lives. And I know that's daft, but that's how I feel, and we can talk to each other about anything.

'What about your boyfriend?' I asked her.

'What boyfriend?'

'When I asked you to go out with me you said you didn't two-time.'

'You idiot! You were the one who was dating. You were with Delfine!'

Bouncing baboon's buttocks! I felt so stupid. I *was* so stupid. I squeezed her hand and asked her what she thought of my white jeans.

'I noticed as soon as you walked in the room,' she said. (So Tasha was right after all! Good for her.) 'And I thought, crap pants but I love him, so what the hell.'

That party proved to be quite an event because Pete asked Tasha to go out with him. He'd had a passion for her as long as I'd had for Sky. That time I'd seen them on the playground, he only wanted to ask Sky how he could get into Tasha's good books.

Dad didn't seem the least bit surprised when Sky started coming round instead of Delfine. He just gave me knowing glances. I could almost hear him thinking: *Ho ho ho. Now he knows what it feels like.* But he didn't say it and I appreciated that.

La Trifle—Tracey—didn't like Sky's hair, which was a bit rich coming from someone who stuck a giant red cherry on top of her head whenever she went out.

'Ignore her,' was Tasha's advice. 'It's a girlie thing.'

141

So things were cool. Tash and I still argued. We still threw things at each other. Pankhurst sometimes attacked me for no good reason and then the next minute she'd be hatching my feet.

And every day I saw Sky.

Miss Kovak was really pleased with the final, finished strip. *All Works* had been a huge success. Even some of the parents had come in to get hold of copies. It wasn't just Sky who was getting asked for autographs—now kids were coming up to me and, guess who? Darcy. He scowled and growled at them, but Sky said that, really, he was chuffed to bits. I examined Darcy's dark face and asked how she could tell.

'By talking to him,' she answered simply.

Even so, it was more than I could bring myself to do. I kept clear of him, just in case.

Pete and I carried on much the same as before. I couldn't help liking him despite all the things he did to wind people up and all the stories he told. I did tackle him about those eventually. 'Tasha reckons you make them up.'

'I do not!'

'Right. So what about the desert story?'

'I went to the desert with my parents,' Pete insisted.

'And you got lost?'

'A bit.'

'And you were rescued by a medicine man?'

'Not exactly. But we did go to the desert and it was very big and we might have got lost.'

'But you didn't?'

'No.'

'And kissing with tongues?'

'Have I done that?' asked Pete in surprise.

142

'So you said. Obviously you haven't.'

'Hmm. Think I might have remembered if I had.'

'You said it was like eating liver without the onions.'

'Disgusting! Don't do it, Stuff. Listen to my warning. If it's like that, you mustn't do it.'

I smiled and thought: *too late,* chum! And it wasn't liver and onions at all. It was champagne and caviar! 'And Aunt Polly's car? Have you ever driven it?' I went on.

'I sat in the driver's seat.'

'Did you drive?'

Pete gave a sheepish grin. 'I made lots of brrrm-brrrm noises and I did a handbrake turn—an imaginary one—but it was a very good imaginary one.'

'Pete?'

'Yes?'

'You're a wozzer.'

'Thank you very much. I refute it, thus.'

He kicked me. How my life goes.